Glimmer In A Glass Eye

Axel Hatchett Mystery Vol. 2

Steven LeRoy Nelson

BLOOD AND THUNDER PRESS

BLOOD AND THUNDER PRESS
3612 Sheffield Lane
Colorado Springs, CO 80907
www.bloodandthunderpress.com

ISBN: 1940469023
ISBN: 978-1-940469-02-7

To my little day-old éclair....

1

I was on the office phone with my mechanic, Otto. I used to love the guy. He took a pretty hot 1951 Hudson Hornet, souped it up, and turned it into a snarling road eater. I was pretty sure he had to dabble in the dark arts to accomplish this, but how a guy does his job is his business. Then Otto got cocky. He started mixing up home-brewed engine additives in some cave somewhere. He filled my Hornet's crankcase with one of these elixirs and froze up the entire engine. He took my swell ride and transformed it into a giant paperweight.

"That buggy of mine about ready?" I said into the mouthpiece.

"You kidding?" Otto had a gravelly voice, like he needed an oil change. "I got to take down the whole engine. It'll take days."

"Days? Look, I need my car back. I'm a private investigator, remember? I can't be tailing cars on foot. I'll burn my shoes up."

"Days, I'm telling you. Maybe by the end of the week. I got a lot of jobs. I'm a popular guy."

"Sure. Life of the party. How about giving me a loaner?"

"I don't have one. I already told you that. Why don't you go rent one?"

"Six dollars a day? I'm a detective, not a diamond broker. What's in that stuff you doped my car with, anyway?"

"Ah, I can't tell you. It's a secret formula."

"Yeah? You should have kept it a secret from yourself. I'll give you three days, then I'm calling the Better Business Bureau."

"Hey, that ain't fair. I've always done right by you, ain't I?"

"Sure, until you turned my Hornet into a boat anchor. That car's only five years old. Why'd you have to mess with it?"

"A guy's got to try new stuff. Stale mechanics don't make the grade. They just get old and greasy."

"You been reading Poor Richard's Almanac again? Three days. That's all I'm giving you. And no more experiments. I'm getting tired of riding the bus to work."

I hung up, then stared at my office door. I was just daring some rube to come on in and hire me. And what do you know? A guy walked in like he owned the place. It was my landlord.

I took a quick peek at my desk calendar. It said, "Three."

"The check is in the mail, Mr. LeFever."

It wasn't really. It was still in my checkbook, not filled out. But details aren't always important.

"Hot in here," LeFever complained, dropping into one of my painful client's chairs. He reached to loosen his tie, but he wasn't wearing one. "Why don't you open the window, turn on that fan? Honest to Crazy Godfrey, it's only September."

"Who's Crazy Godfrey, an uncle?"

"Naw, I just don't like to swear."

I walked over to the window. Not much of a view. In fact, it was painted over. I wrestled it open, then set the fan in it and turned it on. It was a fan any little girl would have loved. Just the right size to put in one of her dollhouse windows.

"Why didn't you do that sooner?" LeFever was shuffling out of his sulfur yellow sports coat now, hanging it on the back of his chair.

"I was trying to keep out the sickly-sweet stench of ice cream toppings," I explained. My office is not only stuffy and low-ceilinged, it's located above a Mom and Pop ice cream parlor. I've always hated ice cream. Cold, slimy stuff, like something you'd make out of snakes. Even as a kid I hated it. When the ice cream truck slithered through our neighborhood, with its cheap, tinny, music, and its stink of pistachio, I'd chase it just to throw rocks at it. An old Model T truck, painted up like a floozy, with Old Man Fribbins driving it like he was having a great time. When he finally died, I was happy to go to his funeral.

"You don't like ice cream toppings?" LeFever was back sitting in his chair, and was fiddling with a pencil he'd taken off my desk.

"Long story, never mind. How can I help you? Like I said, I mailed your check. Maybe the damned stamp fell off. The kind of glue they use is a travesty."

He waved an impatient hand.

"Never mind that. I'm here to hire you."

I got back to my desk and slumped in my squeaky chair. I took a yellow legal pad from a desk drawer and motioned for LeFever to give me back my pencil. He did so, reluctantly. I took a good look at the guy. He was my landlord all right. Gray crew cut, poorly shaven jowls, a complexion the color of old bricks with an underlying purplish tint. Stop snacking on rock salt, I thought. It ain't good for your blood pressure. What I said out loud was, "You need a detective? Tell me your story."

He reached up and unbuttoned the top button of his gray-and-yellow-checked short-sleeved shirt. There were gray hairs on the back of his meaty hand. Sweat was beginning to slide down his temples like drool from a hound's mouth.

"You ought to invest in air conditioning," he said.

"You told me when I rented the place that it was well insulated, and that it was nice and cool in the summer."

"Did I? I was going by what the last tenant told

4

me. Guy must have been from the Sahara. In fact, come to think of it — ″

I held my hand up to stop him. Just like a used car dealer; he could spin a lie with the best of them, but I kept the thought to myself. I can be tactful when there's money in it. Dobie LeFever, of Lefever's Used Car Gems. From what I'd seen of them, they were more like used car rhinestones. But I didn't mention that either.

"Tell me why you need a gumshoe."

"Some guy tried to drown me."

"That so? A happy customer? Did you go to the police?"

He shook his head.

"No. No cops. I've got my reasons. Guy tried to drown me. I can't swim, and I think he knew that."

"He knew you? Where did this happen, and when?"

"Up by my place, my home. We live in Topaz Canyon. You know it?"

"Sure. In the mountains. There are some nice houses up there."

"Yeah, but the road can be hell in the winter. Most of us drive trucks, or Jeeps."

"And this was when?"

"Couple of days ago. Guy tried to drown me."

"We covered that."

"Sure. There's a small lake, about half-a-mile from our house, right next to the road. I take the dog out walking there about every day. When I get home from work. After dinner."

"What kind of dog?"

"Does it matter?"

"How should I know? Maybe."

"A black Scotty named Sinbad."

I wrote it down. "So you're walking down by the lake. What time? Around dusk?"

"A little later. Almost dark. The lake's got a little dock for fishermen and boats. I walked out to the end of it with the dog to look at the water, watch the fish jump. Next thing I knew, somebody came up from behind and pushed us in the lake. Well, he pushed me in the lake. The dog got pulled in because I didn't let go of his leash. I sunk like a rock, but I managed to splash around enough to get to the surface and grab onto the dock. I thought I was OK, then the guy — it was dark by now and I couldn't see him much — grabbed me and started trying to duck me under again. I thought I was a goner. Then I saw this bright light on the lake."

"An angel?" I wrote down, 'Guardian angel.' It looked swell next to 'Sinbad. Black Scotty.'

"What? An angel? Honest to Crazy Godfrey. No, a car. A car came driving by on the road with its lights on. It must have scared my attacker. He ran off, and I was able to pull myself up onto the dock. I was soaking wet, and shaking."

"What about the dog?"

"Him? He swam out on his own and high-tailed it home. When I got there, Rolaine was drying him off with a bath towel. Rolaine, that's my wife."

"The wife doesn't go on the walks with you?"

"Can't. She's got a condition. Can't stand open spaces. They call it something."

"Agoraphobia."

"Smart guy! Right. Agoraphobia. Tough break for her."

"Could you identify this attacker if you saw him again?"

"No. Like I said, he snuck up behind me. And the second time, when he ducked me, it was already too dark to see."

"You suggested the guy might know you because he knew you couldn't swim. Who do you have for enemies? I mean, you're a used car dealer."

"LeFever's Used Car Gems are just that. Gems. I make friends, not enemies."

He was turning even redder. I let that line of questioning go.

"OK, who else? Who besides a customer might want you dead?"

"I think I might know who did it, but I want you to prove it. Here, I might be able to help you." He reached around to his jacket on his chair back and fished in an inside pocket. He pulled out something wrapped in waxed paper and handed it to me. "Watch out for fingerprints."

"Fingerprints don't mean anything to me."

The parcel was about six inches long, two wide, and maybe an inch thick. I unwrapped it. What I found was a pair of men's eyeglasses with brown plastic frames. They looked pretty new. The lenses were thick. This guy probably couldn't see a thing without his glasses. I wondered how he'd driven home, or if driving had been necessary. On the inside of one temple was a narrow decal that said "Vision Quest." I knew the place — a small optical shop downtown.

"You said you might know the guy who dunked you in the lake. How so?"

"Let me explain. It's a long story."

"I think I've got the time."

"It goes all the way back to high school."

"I'm listening."

He took his show hanky out of his jacket pocket. It was gray with yellow checks in shades that kind of matched his shirt. He used it to mop his crew cut and his jowls. It wasn't a show hanky any more. God knows it was hot enough in my little haven, but not that hot.

"My wife, Rolaine, was a cheerleader in high school. She was a looker, let me tell you. Still is. She's my age, but you'd never guess she was near forty. Anyhow, all the boys were after her, including me. But there was this other kid, a bad boy named Stu Slaughter. His folks didn't have much money, but Stu bought this old motorcycle, an Indian, and he fixed it up and painted it red. He rode it all over the place, and he rode it fast."

"Is the speed at which young Slaughter rode his bike important to this case?"

"Hey, you're the one who asked what kind of dog I had."

"Point taken. Go on."

"Stu's Uncle Milo was kind of a hillbilly. He had a still out in the woods someplace. Stu sold some of the moonshine to the high school boys and kept part of the profits, which meant he had money in his pocket most of the time. He was bad, like I said. Played hooky, got in fights, got drunk, and rode around on that noisy Indian all the time. Rolaine fell for him like a ton of bricks. Explain that to me! Why do good girls fall for bad boys?"

"I don't know anything about dames, no matter what their age."

"Well, her folks weren't any too happy about it. They were kind of churchy."

"I'm sure Uncle Milo was saddened by that."

"Maybe so. Rolaine had to see Stu on the sly, but all the kids knew they were boyfriend and girlfriend. And then this bad girl moved to town. The whole family was rotten. Shiftless."

"Don't tell me... the bad girl fell for a good boy. You're making me cry."

"No. She fell for Stu, and he liked her. A match made by the Devil."

"He sure does get around."

"Quit butting in. Honest to Crazy Godfrey it's hot in here. I want to get out as soon as I can."

"Maybe we can talk about your lowering the rent."

"What? No. You're getting the place cheap.

Look at all the space you've got."

"I'm not a piano dealer. I don't need the space."

"Getting back to what I was telling you. Stu ends up dumping Rolaine. Hard. She bounced."

"Most cute cheerleaders do. All right, you win, tell the story straight through and I promise I won't interrupt."

"Thanks. Rolaine took it bad. I was right there to help her."

"Kind of you."

"Listen, you just said — "

"I know. My fat lips are sealed. Go on."

"I knew a good chance when I saw one. I did everything I could to make Rolaine my girl. I was on the football team: third string punter. I pumped gas after school for a few bucks, so I had some cash. I think at first she just went along with it. You know, she was hoping Stu would think she didn't care about him anymore. But after a while she actually began liking me. Pretty soon we were going steady. And then you know what happened?"

"You knocked her up?"

"No! Listen, you said — "

"You asked me a question!"

"OK. Here's what happened: the bad girl and her family skipped town. They left a whole lot of unpaid bills behind, and damned if Stu didn't start making up to Rolaine."

"I thought you told me you don't like to curse."

"Honest to Crazy Godfrey! Are all peepers like

you?"

"No comment."

"It looked to me like Rolaine was all ready to go back to her bad boy. Nearly drove me nuts. I decided I had to do something. I had an old Model-T I drove, and I had a jar of Milo's corn squeezin's I'd been saving for graduation, to celebrate. I got pretty liquored up and drove over to Stu's house to give him what for. He was out in the yard, chopping wood. Nobody else was home. We got into it good. Stu had a reputation for being a tough fighter, and I found out why. I thought he was going to kill me. Good thing I was too drunk to feel any pain. He kept knocking me down, and somehow I kept getting back up. Finally, I got in one good punch, and boy was it a doozy. Is that cursing?"

"Doozy? I've heard priests use it."

"OK. I had this ring I'd made in metal shop class. A big lump of brass, like a brass knuckle. I was wearing it that day. When I got in my good punch, that ring ruined his eye. I mean, ruined it. He had to have it taken out later. I'll never forgive myself."

"You're serious? You blinded him in one eye?"

He nodded, then wiped down his head with the ex-show hanky again. For a moment I thought he was crying, but it was just sweat.

"Stu's folks could have sued my folks, but suing wasn't as popular back then as it is now."

"Must have been tough on lawyers. You know,

Mr. LeFever, this happened when you were just a kid. It was an accident. Quit beating yourself up over it."

"I wish I could. At the time I didn't know what to do. All I could think of was to give him back Rolaine. But — wouldn't you know it? — she wouldn't have anything to do with him. She stuck to me like glue."

What happened to Slaughter?"

"Him? He dropped out of high school. We were only a few weeks away from graduation, but he dropped out. He tried to join the Marines. No luck. They wouldn't take a guy with only one eye. So, he went off to Africa, to Kenya. Stu had always been a pretty good shot, and he still had the eye he aimed with. He went to work for some safari outfit, shooting meat to feed the safari hunters. After a while he got a job as a safari guide.

"He disappeared from our lives for years. Rolaine and me, three months after high school, we got hitched. We've been living in Topaz Canyon for a couple of years now. About a year ago, Stu moved back to Quartz Quarry. His folks still live here. He got hurt while he was in Africa. One of his customers wounded an elephant and Stu had to finish it off, but it trampled him a little first. So, now he's got a bad back. In a way, I blame myself."

"I'd blame the elephant."

"His heath's not perfect, but he can still work as a local hunting guide. He's started his own business. And guess what? He started renting a house in Topaz Canyon that me and Rolaine own as an investment. He didn't know who the owner was when he moved in — I let a management company take care of things like that. When I found out who was renting it, I called him and offered to give him a break on the rent. Nothing doing. He'll never let me do anything to sort of make up for what I did. I guess he's doing all right helping folks hunt elk and bear. And he's got his snakes."

"Snakes! What are you telling me?"

2

"He keeps a bunch of rattlesnakes in his garage. I'm not even sure if that's legal, but I leave him alone about it. He sells their venom to the local college, and some to a vet in town who uses horses to make some kind of snakebite cure. Think of that — horses! But, you know, lately I haven't been feeling as charitable towards Stu as I used to."

"Let me guess. You think he's been sleeping with your wife."

"You guessed right."

"And you think that he wants you out of the way, and so he tried to drown you."

"That's how I see it. It could also be he wants to get back at me for blinding one of his eyes."

"Hold on a minute. That doesn't make sense. If Slaughter wanted you out of the way, and maybe your wife wants that too, then there's such a thing as divorce. As for the getting even angle, why wait all this time? I know he's been off in Africa, but you said he's been back here for a year."

"Yeah, well, I think Africa might have quite a bit to do with his trying to kill me. I mean, face it, it's full of wild animals and savages. Folks out in the jungle don't see things like we do here. We're civilized. I think Stu kind of went native. He might be able to bump me off without thinking a thing of it. What do you think?"

"I think it's a lot of hooey. By the way, 'hooey' isn't a curse word either. Ask the Pope."

"Well, maybe you don't agree with my ideas, but I still want you to help me get to the bottom of things."

"I'll do what I can. But let me ask you something. I gather you think these glasses belong to Slaughter. Where'd you get them?"

"I found them on the pier when I crawled out. They must've fallen off the attacker's face when he was trying to duck me. I think they're Stu's because, like I told you, I believe he's the guy who tried to drown me."

"Have you looked through the lenses of these glasses?"

"No. My Mom always told me not to look through other people's spectacles. She said it could ruin my eyes."

"I'm glad you're a good boy and listen to your mother. My Mom never told me a damn thing about anybody's glasses, and so I went ahead and looked through these. The lenses are thick, both of them. Since Slaughter's blind in one eye, why would he need high-powered lenses for both eyes?"

That made him scratch his head.

"Are you telling me he's not blind in one eye?"

"I'm not telling you anything of the kind. I'm telling you that the guy who wears these glasses might not be blind in one eye. Maybe somebody else shoved you into the lake."

"Then how's come he knew I couldn't swim?"

"Maybe he didn't. Maybe he was just hoping. Or maybe he just wanted to get a kick out of seeing someone flail around in the water."

"Maybe. But you're taking the case?"

"Of course I'm taking the case. And I'm going to try to find out who these spectacles belong to. I'm just saying it might not be Stu Slaughter."

"Well, that's OK. I just want to know."

"Fine. Let's talk money since I do this for a living. Let's talk contract."

That made him squirm in his chair. He scratched his head again. He even tried to refold his handkerchief so it would look like something other than a mechanic's shop rag when he stuffed it back into his pocket. It didn't work. He gave up and stuffed it into his back pants pocket instead.

"I don't really think you and me need a contract. Do you? I mean, you already owe me rent. How about I pay you that way? A couple of month's rent."

"No. But before we go any farther, I've got to tell you something. I don't have a car."

"They repossessed your car? Things are that bad? I'm beginning to think you can't be much of a detective."

"Nobody repossessed my car. I still own it, but it's in the shop. My mechanic poured some kind of homemade molasses into my crankcase. It's not running. I'll have it back in two or three days. I could rent a car, but I think my mechanic should pay for it, and he won't. I'm talking about a matter of principle."

"If you don't have a car, then you need a loaner." He laughed suddenly, raucously, and a crow outside answered him. "I'm a used car dealer. I could loan you a hundred cars."

"One will do. I guess you can loan it to me for free."

"I guess not. Five bucks a day. That's a buck less than a regular car rental place would charge. Add that to the two month's rent I'm letting you slide out of, and I think we've got a deal."

"How about if I keep the car permanently and promise to work really hard for you?"

He fidgeted in his chair.

"Hey, let's do things like gentlemen — everything under the table. No cash. Two-and-a-half month's rent and I'll loan you a really swell auto. A cream puff. Your choice of colors. Huh?"

"No. How about you forgive two-and-a-half month's rent, loan me an ordinary car that runs, and add two- hundred dollars retainer?"

"What are you going to do with two- hundred

bucks? Drink champagne on the job? Swill caviar?"

"You don't swill caviar. It's not a liquid. I need a retainer as a goodwill gesture on your part, and to pay for meals, gas, bribes and other expenses related to the job."

"I'll give you a hundred bucks."

"Make it a hundred-and-fifty and I'll smile really big for you."

"OK. Deal. You drive a hard bargain."

"I'm getting robbed. Let me draw up a contract."

"Come on, a handshake will do."

"Your hand? I'll type up a nice simple contract."

"A handshake, or I walk."

I made some pretty dramatic sighing noises, but not good enough to get me a job in the theatre. I needed money. I needed work. Nobody was offering but Dobie LeFever. He had me over a barrel — the kind filled with water and sharks.

"Done. Give me the hundred-and-fifty bucks, and I'll get right to work for you."

He smiled with yellow teeth, worked a packet of cigarettes out of his shirt pocket, and then lit one with a nice gold Zippo he took from his pants.

"I've been saving this," he said. "Rolaine wants me to cut back on my smoking. Women. Like cigarettes ever hurt anybody!" He stood up and exchanged a handshake with the dumb shamus, then he dug a business card out of his wallet and gave it to me. "Both my business and my home numbers are on it. Call me when you know something. Anything."

"What about the car?"

"Oh, yeah. What make do you like?"

"It doesn't matter. Something plain. Brown or gray, if possible. No dents or other distinguishing marks. It'd be nice if it had something under the hood."

"I got a dozen jalopies just like that. I'll pick one out and send it over as soon as I get back to the lot. It should be here in less than an hour."

"Fill it up before you send it over, will you?"

"Half a tank. That should do you for a while. If you need more gas, use your retainer."

"Speaking of which."

"Yeah, yeah, I got it."

He hauled out a showy money clip practically dislocating its jaw on a big wad of bills. He counted out a hundred-and-fifty dollars and handed it to me.

"Good luck, amigo. Call me when you find something out."

He put on his coat and left my office the way he'd come in. Like he owned the place.

3

After LeFever left, I spent some time sitting at my desk, thinking. I'm pretty good at it. Sitting, I mean. I wasn't sure how I could discover who had tried to kill my client, but the best place to start was Vision Quest. As soon as my loaner car arrived, I planned to drive over to the optical shop and talk to someone. Maybe more than one someone.

In less than an hour, I heard an impatient honking down in the little parking lot I shared with the ice cream parlor. I stuck my head out the door and saw two cars parked near the foot of the outside stairs. Two men stood outside of them. One was a small, plain, little rat of a man, the other was big and bluff, with a showy ice-blue sports coat with white piping along the lapels. The cars resembled the drivers. One, the jalopy I assumed was meant for me, was a several-years-old Chevy, brown in color and plain as a West Virginia school marm. The other car looked like a cross between a fire engine and a yacht. It was an early-fifties Nash Ambassador, crimson red.

"Hey, your car's here," the big guy shouted up at me. "She's a doozy."

"Stop cursing, I just got out of church." He didn't know what to do with that. I started down the stairs.

"It's perfect," I said, taking a long gander at the Chevy.

"Wrong car, bub," Big Guy said.

Up close I could see what he was trying to be. The big smile, the broad gestures, the hale-fellow-well-met ring to his voice. He was posing as an aw shucks, regular guy, happy as a pig full of mashed potatoes and gravy. But his eyes gave him away. They were the color of old ice, and just as friendly.

"Are you trying to unload this Nash on me?"

"Unload?" he snarled, like I had just said something about his sister that was true. "This boat's a beaut. Thinking of buying it myself. And I want you should take care of it. How's about you show some appreciation?"

I smiled big, jumped up in the air and tried to click my heels three times. I only got two clicks. "Like that?"

"Smart guy, huh?" With great reluctance he handed me a red leather key fob with a gold "N" stamped on it. Attached to the fob were two silvery keys.

"You serious? I told your boss I wanted something inconspicuous. Not the Queen Mary all tricked out for Christmas. Let me have the Chevy. It's perfect."

"Glad you love it. If it was up to me, that's exactly the car you'd get. But LeFever likes you. He wants you to have something special."

"Tell him I liked the Chevy better."

"Nope. Boss's orders, pal. It's the Nash or nothing."

I thought about it. I was starting to fume. Big Guy could probably smell it on my breath. He smiled, using more than his fair share of teeth.

"I've said my last word," he told me.

I doubted that. I squinted at the Nash, heaved a sigh. Hell, maybe I could find a mud hole to paint it with.

"OK. Thanks for bringing me the car. Thank LeFever for me. I'll take care of the Super Chief for you, don't worry."

"That's better." He sounded almost friendly again. He stuck out a hand the size of a welcome mat. "Travis Spencer. Sales Manager for LeFever's Used Car Gems. Pleased to meet you." He gave me his patented honest woodchopper's handshake. My finger bones melded and my hand turned into a flipper. "I didn't catch your name."

"Axe Hatchett."

"For real?"

"As I live and breathe."

He laughed. It sounded like a walrus impersonating a hog caller. He turned to his sidekick. "Let's me and you go, Andy. I'm driving."

They piled into the nice dull Chevy and I wistfully waved it goodbye.

I climbed the stairs to my office to lock up. While I was there, I fetched the glasses LeFever had given me. I turned off the baby fan and took it out of the window, then I closed the window and latched it. It was hot, but heat was better than the stink of ice cream and its accouterments.

I went downstairs and climbed into the Nash and fiddled with its gadgets and gizmos. The car had everything. Power steering, power brakes, power windows. The best of radios. Even an automatic transmission and air conditioning, honest to Crazy Godfrey! The front seats reclined all the way flat, and — in combination with the backseat — made a big bed nicer than the one I spend most nights in. I fired up the baby and pointed its winged hood ornament in the direction of downtown. Vision Quest, here I come!

The optical store was housed in a one-story brick building painted white. Beside it was a small parking lot. I docked the Nash between a green Studebaker pick-up truck and an old Army Jeep that someone had painted black and spent a lot of time on making more mountain worthy. The day was bright and sunny, dusty smelling, and the sky was as blue as the ocean is green.

I went through the front door of Vision Quest and was assaulted by too much air conditioning. It was a pretty little place. Beige carpeting, maple wall shelves with a clutter of eyeglass frames on them, and quite an assortment of rock crystals, likely from local sources, to give the shop some color. A young woman wearing a blue blazer, lighter blue slacks, and a white blouse came over and asked if she could help me.

"I'm Ann," she said in a voice that was somehow both chirpy and sultry. "You look like a man who could use a new pair of glasses."

"Only so I could see you better." She wasn't pretty in a conventional way, but she used what she had. A round figure, medium-brown hair cut short, way too many freckles, and a pair of lavender eyes that made the whole package worth looking at. "Actually, if you'll believe it, I don't wear glasses."

She laughed, a fulsome tinkle, like I'd said something really witty.

"So, you're one of those handsome men who's afraid glasses will spoil his looks. You've come to the right place. We have frames that will make you look even more distinguished than you do already. With the right glasses, you might make a girl like me lose her head."

"I'm too old for you, but if you're nice I might let you hold my store-bought teeth."

She gave me the laugh again.

"I like the touch of gray in your hair. We have some lovely gray frames, in durable plastic."

"Probably more durable than I am. Listen, I'm really not here for spectacles. I need some help with a different matter." I slipped the pair of glasses out of my inside jacket pocket. I'd ditched the waxed paper. "I need to find the guy who lost these."

She gave me a confused frown.

"It's a long story. Maybe I need to tell it to a manager. I see you have other customers."

There were, in fact, other customers. An elderly couple had just walked in and they were both stumbling around like they'd accidentally left their seeing eye dog at home.

"Maybe you're right," Ann said. "I'll get my brother. He's in the lab." She turned to the elderly couple and shouted, "I'm Ann. I'll be right with you."

She left me, but I consoled myself with the view of her retreating posterior. I looked around the shop some more. There were some sunglasses I thought I might be interested in, but then I looked at the price. In a couple of minutes a swinging door at the back squeaked open and ejected a stocky man in a white lab coat. His hair was darker than his sister's, and he probably had to shave more often. In fact, he had the look of a guy whose five-o'clock shadow starts somewhere around ten in the morning.

He came up to me, smiling, and stuck out a stubby paw. I shook it. A nametag on his coat declared him to be one P.D. Slabov. A second line said he was the owner/lab manager.

"How can I be of service," he asked, in a burly baritone. His eyes weren't lavender, like Ann's.

They were pinkish-gray, like a sick bunny's.

"Dr. Slabov?"

"I can't accept the compliment," he giggled richly. "I'm not a doctor. Call me P.D. And your name?"

I've noticed in the past that people aren't always forthcoming if they know they're talking to a private investigator. They get nervous. So, sometimes I don't tell them. I make up an alias, and a fake profession.

"My name's Eustace Waldengarver. Gourmet tapioca salesman."

"Fascinating."

"I've got a little problem, and I hope that you can solve it." I handed him the glasses. "I see by the label on those that they came from this shop."

"So they did, yes. This is one of our more popular frames. How did you come by them?"

"There's a story behind that. You up to listening to a little tale of woe and rescue?"

"I can spare a few minutes, yes."

"Yesterday, I was up in Topaz Canyon, just driving around, and it started raining. My poor old Henry J got stuck right up to the axels. I tried pushing it out of the mud, but I didn't have the strength.

"Fortunately, another motorist showed up and gave me a hand. Big guy, though not young. The two of us were able to get my buggy back on dry ground. I tried to give the guy a tip, but he was too proud to take it. So, I had to settle for just saying thanks. After he left, I walked around the Henry J to make sure it wasn't damaged, and right on top of the trunk lid was laying this pair of glasses. The guy hadn't been wearing them, he'd been wearing sunglasses. These must have slipped out of his shirt pocket when we were giving my bus the old heave-ho. I noticed the lenses were pretty thick.

"I hung around a while, thinking maybe he'd notice he'd lost them and come back, but it didn't happen. And I thought, what a shame. Here this man was nice enough to stop and give me a hand, and what does he get for it? He loses an expensive pair of spectacles. I didn't even know the guy's name. So, I saw that Vision Quest decal on the glasses and I got an idea. I thought maybe my good Samaritan might come in here to get a replacement pair. Has a guy complaining about lost glasses come in today?"

Slabov shook his head sadly. "I'm afraid not. But why don't you leave the glasses here. If he comes in, we'll be able to return them."

"I was just thinking that. I gave out my last business card earlier this morning, so let me just write down my number for you. I'm worried about the guy. If you give me his address I can mail him a little present."

"A sampler of tapioca?"

"You guessed right, pardner. But while I've still got your ear, let me ask you another question. Strictly optical."

"I should be able to answer that one."

"Good. Here goes. I was looking this pair of glasses over. I noticed he's got a pretty strong prescription. Both eyes."

"Yes, he's seriously nearsighted."

"You can tell that just by looking at them?"

"That's my job."

"Well, both lenses are strong. And here's the curious thing. When we were pushing my jalopy out of the buffalo wallow it was stuck in, the guy kind of bumped against me. Just an accident. He apologized and said it was because I was standing on his blind side. Said he'd been blind in one eye since birth. His eye looked OK to me, but he said it didn't work. Now, tell me, why make a strong prescription lens for a blind eye?"

He treated me to his manly giggle again.

"It's called a balance lens. It's made to match the lens for the sighted eye. Purely for cosmetic reasons, you understand. You want the lenses to be the same thickness. There's another reason, too. Lenses made to correct nearsightedness make the eyes look smaller when you're looking at the person wearing them. If you're farsighted, your eyes will appear larger. For instance, if you were wearing glasses right now, and one of your eyes was nearsighted, and the other was farsighted, then when I looked at you your eyes would appear to be two very different sizes. Am I making myself clear?"

"I think I understand. But if that was the case,

then I'd be stuck. You couldn't do anything cosmetically to help me look less screwy. But if I was blind in one eye, you could make that lens match the other, and my eyes would look the same size, if anybody cared to look."

"Precisely. You're a good pupil."

"Tell me, if I came in here without my prescription in my pocket, and I wore glasses, is there some kind of machine you could use to read my prescription off my specs?"

"Yes, there is such a machine. I have two of them. They're called vertometers."

"Sure they are. Any chance you could read the prescription off this Samaritan's glasses and look him up in your records?"

"Nice idea, but, no. Our records are set up by the customer's name. And since you don't know the fellow's name — "

"Got you. Well, listen, thanks for letting me use up so much of your time. If that guy comes in here, looking for a new pair of glasses, give me a ring. Huh?"

"Certainly. I'll be happy to. And let's hope he does show up."

"Let's" I glanced at my watch. "Jeez, I've been having such a good conversation with you that I've let the time slip by. I've got to head over to the Tapioca Convention at the hotel. We're going to sing songs, wear funny hats, and talk cassava starch. It's good for the morale. Life can get lonely on the road."

I left, waving at Ann as I went out. She was still helping the elderly couple. She threw me a wink.

I went out the door feeling like I'd wasted my time. All I'd learned was that the glasses could possibly belong to Stew Slaughter. That was something, but not much.

4

Back in the Nash — I felt like I should be wearing a Commodore's hat — I headed the boat in the direction of Rocko's Kitchen. It was lunch time, and I wanted a burger and fries, and a chat with one of Rocko's waitresses.

When I reached the diner, I parked the Nash Ambassador Golden Airflyte, for such was my vehicle, right in front. The diner's blinds were still closed to keep out the morning sun. I went inside. and the counter girl, Tracy, smiled at me with her big bright teeth. I'm the only customer she smiles for. She turned her face and offered me a chaste cheek. I kissed it. She's my girlfriend, but she hasn't been for long.

"Hamburger and fries coming right up," she said. "I'll make some fresh coffee."

"While the food's cooking, why not come out and take a gander at the submarine I'm navigating."

"You got your Hornet back?"

"I wish. Come look."

That was a mistake. Tracy fell in love with the car. I thought she was going to try to eat it.

"It's the reddest car I've ever seen," she said. "It's gorgeous. It's like a rolling work of art. Mona Lisa with training wheels. Where'd you get this beauty? Savings Stamps?"

"It's a loaner from a guy who's my client."

"You're working again? That's great! Does that mean you can pay for your burger and fries?"

"Ask me after I've eaten."

We went back inside and I ate my lunch, wiped the grease off my chin, and had a second cup of coffee. And the whole time, Tracy talked about the car.

"What does a dream like that cost?"

"More than a kid like you can afford."

"But it's used."

"So is the Taj Mahal. Care to make an offer? Where would you drive it, anyway? You never go anyplace."

"Drive it? Are you crazy? I'd live in it."

"I'll find out from LeFever what he wants for it. Though his sales manager is hot to trot to buy it."

"I've been saving all my tips for three years."

"You think a buck-eighty is going to buy a car like that?"

"Smart guy. I get tips. Not everybody's a cheapo like you."

On my way home I stopped by my office again. I made a phone call to a guy named Bram Duckers. He's the only guy I use as an operative, and lately I haven't had much of anything for him. Or me. He works full time at the Happy Trails Shooting Range, has a pregnant wife, Celeste, and a fat mortgage on a broken-down duplex. He and Celeste live on one side, and the other side is being fixed up for a rental.

I wanted to talk to Bram about the goat man case. Some old geezer in the country thought his neighbor's dogs were jumping the fence and worrying his goats so much they were giving sour milk. I put Bram on the case. He's been watching the dogs when he's not working at Happy Trails.

I got Bram on the phone and he told me the goat geezer had it all wrong. The dogs weren't jumping the fence, the goats were. They were chasing the poor hounds around the yard and then going back home. If the goats were giving bad milk it was because they had rotten personalities.

I quit talking to Bram and dialed the goat man's number. He didn't like what I had to say. He asked for his retainer back, and said he wouldn't pay me another dime. I told him I'd just saved him a ton of money. If he'd gone after his neighbors they would have proved him wrong and sued him for dog harassment. On top of that, if he didn't pay me what he owed me, I'd have my lawyer go after him until he started giving sour milk himself. I got him to come around to my view, we haggled over the fee, and he promised to send me a check.

I hoped he would.

I tried to call LeFever at work to tell him the attacker might in fact be Slaughter, in spite of the glasses. He wasn't at the main lot, so I tried the other one. They told me he'd been there but had left around noon to take care of a personal matter. I thought I might try him at home later. I headed home myself. What else did I have to do?

About seven the next morning my phone rang, It was my girl, Tracy.

"I didn't wake you, did I, Turnip Head?"

"No. I'm drinking my second cup of coffee. And it's better than the stuff you make."

"Aren't you sweet. You must have seen the morning paper."

"I don't get the paper delivered anymore. I can't afford it."

"There's bad news in it for you. I think you're out of a job. That guy you told me about, Dobie LeFever. He's dead."

"What? That can't be. Drowned?"

"No, worse. Or, I guess it's about the same. He got bit by a big rattlesnake. Died on the way to the hospital."

"A rattler? Tell me it was a wild one, please."

"I can't. It was in a cage in somebody's garage. Actually, it wasn't in its cage. It got out. It bit the used car guy in the leg."

"It sounds like it was one of Stu Slaughter's snakes. First he tried to drown poor Dobie, and then he sicced a snake on him. I wish I could prove it, but that's up to the cops And I'm not even on anyone's payroll now."

"I'm sorry, Briar Patch. So, what's going to happen to that swell car now?"

"It'll go back to the lot. That reminds me, I need to call my mechanic and threaten him some more."

"I didn't even get to ride in the Ruby Roadrunner."

"That's what you call it?"

"A car like that's got to have a name."

"Listen, I'll drop by Rocko's before I return the Nash. You can get Cookie to watch the counter while I take you for a spin."

"I can't go joy riding. I've got to work."

"Rocko doesn't deserve you."

"Haven't I told you? There's no Rocko. Cookie owns the place."

"I'll be damned. What's his real name?"

"Calvin Corsica. Italian, I think."

"Yeah? Well, tell Calvin I'm coming over to give you the ride of your life. Tell him if he's not willing to watch the counter in his own diner for a few minutes, I'll send a meat inspector over to investigate his meatloaf."

"He'd have a heart attack. Then I'd be out of work. OK. I'll tell him something. I'll remind him he hasn't paid me my Christmas bonus for three years running."

When I got to Rocko's, I glided to the curb and honked. While I waited, I thought of LeFever. Jeez,

I couldn't believe he was dead. It wasn't my fault, but I couldn't help but feel guilty. If I'd somehow acted sooner, Dobie might still be alive. Maybe I shouldn't have gone home so early yesterday. I should have driven up to Topaz Canyon and found Slaughter's house and dropped sinister hints about certain persons dunking certain other persons into lakes. At least it might have slowed him down, kept him from arranging for LeFever to die by snakebite.

Tracy finally escaped Rocko's and I took her for a short ride around the neighborhood. I offered to let her drive, but she demurred.

"It'd be like driving the Parthenon, or something," she said. "If I wrecked it, all those snooty art lovers would hate me. And you know how they can be."

"Yeah. Besides, the Parthenon probably has a shorter turning radius."

When we got back to Rocko's, Tracy tearfully patted the Nash goodbye. I headed for the office.

I sat at my desk a while, hoping a client would show up. One didn't. I made a quick call to my mechanic. After about a dozen rings, he answered.

"Otto's Autos. This is Otto speaking."

"Who else would be speaking? You're a one-man garage."

"New customers don't know that. I could have an army of grease monkeys for all folks know."

"You do enough damage all by yourself. How's the Hornet? All well again? Can I come pick it

GLIMMER IN A GLASS EYE

up?"

"I got the engine all torn down. I'm cleaning every part like I was a surgeon."

"Thank God you aren't. Finish your spitting and polishing and get my wheels up and running again. You hear me?"

"Yeah, yeah, I hear you. Think I got nothing to do but work on your car?"

"Make it a priority. You're killing me, Otto. I need my ride back."

"Yeah? Well if I didn't have to spend hours and hours talking to you on the phone, I might be able to do my job."

"Has it really been hours? How time flies. I thought I'd called you less than five minutes ago. Guess I was enjoying your witty and effervescent conversation so much the time just flew. I'll call you tomorrow, and I want the car done. Stay up until three in the morning if you have to." I hung up.

I'd scarcely put the phone back on its cradle when it started ringing.

"Hatchett's Investigations. No nut too hard to crack. Axe speaking"

"I got a nut for you to crack. When you going to drop off that Nash?"

"Mr. Spencer? Nice hearing from you. Come get the car yourself. Delivery was never part of the deal. Are those tears I hear in your voice? You must be pretty broken-up with your boss dying and all."

"I regret his passing deeply. Drive that car right over here, main lot. And put some gas in it first."

"Now you're talking like an idiot. I've got half a mind to call the widow LeFever and ask her to let me keep the car a while. I'm not through with my investigation."

"He's dead. What's to investigate?"

"Oh, there's the little matter of looking into that snakebite accident. Maybe a couple of other things. What do you know about what I was hired for?"

"Dobie had a big mouth. He told me all about being thrown in the lake. And he hired you to find out who did it. Any luck?"

"It's none of your damned business. Now, please excuse me while I hang up on you. I'm expecting an important call. It concerns Girl Scout cookies. How many boxes do you think I should get?"

I slammed down the phone. I waited for Spencer to call back. He did.

"OK. I'm coming to get the car. Don't go anyplace." He hung up. What rude telephone manners.

I had a dartboard in my office. I decided to use it. After I'd thrown my fourth bulls eye, out of about a thousand throws, I heard a car horn honking downstairs. I made sure I had the keys for the Nash and stepped out onto the landing. The old brown Chevy was back, but Travis Spencer was conspicuous by his absence. In his place were two polite lot boys. They called me sir, and expressed the hope that I'd enjoyed the car. Travis could have learned a lot from them.

"I don't suppose I could give you a few bucks to let me have that broken down Chevy for a while?"

"No, sir. You'd have to talk to the sales manager, Mr. Spencer. He's in charge now. Now that — Mr. LeFever's no longer with us." I thought the kid was going to cry.

"The Chevrolet's not broken down, sir," the other kid told me. "It runs like a top."

I gnashed my teeth. I hoped they didn't hear.

"All right, here's the keys to the Nash. Accept my condolences for the loss of Mr. LeFever." Now both of them looked like they were going to cry.

They each climbed into a car and I watched their rear ends until they were out of sight. The cars' rear ends. I realized, to my surprise, that I was going to miss the Nash, and not just because I needed wheels. The Ambassador was a pain to drive in some ways. It yawed on the curves like a carnival ride, and because of its size — and the idiotic front fender skirts — you needed a space a little larger than Arizona to make a U-turn. Also, when I pushed the gas pedal to the floor, its acceleration proved a bit sedate. Still, it had a certain charm. And Tracy loved it. I climbed the outside steps to my office, a saddened man.

Three more days passed by. My threats to Otto fell on deaf ears. I took the bus to my office each morning, and in the evening I locked up and took the bus home. Good thing Quartz Quarry has a nice bus system. On the morning of the fourth day, I opened my office door to the sweet sound of my phone ringing. I grabbed it.

"Mr. Hatchett?" The voice was OK. Better than OK. A satiny, girlish, purr. But there was an edge to it.

"This is Rolaine LeFever."

"My condolences, ma'am."

"Thank you. Can you spare a minute?"

"I can spare several."

"I may want to hire you. Or, rehire you. Something disturbing has happened connected with Dobie's death."

"Really? Tell me about it."

"I got a call last evening from a man, or a boy, claiming to be a concerned college student."

"I didn't know there was such a thing." She ignored me.

"A biology major. He wouldn't give me his name, but he sounded sincere. I don't think it was a prank. Did you know they don't perform autopsies in Quartz Quarry?"

"Yeah. They send the stiffs to Denver or one of its suburbs. Oh, sorry."

"Yes, well, my caller is quite interested in reptile poisons. He said he has a friend who works for the medical examiner's office in Denver. He'd been in contact with his friend lately because he was specifically interested in the results of Dobie's

— autopsy." She broke down a bit here, but recovered with speed. "He heard from his friend yesterday. Then he thought about things for a while and called me. I guess the results don't make a lot of sense. Dobie was killed by an eight-foot-long diamondback rattlesnake. It's venom is mostly a hemotoxin. It works on the blood. I made notes, like a silly schoolgirl.

"According to my caller, Dobie should likely have bled to death internally. The venom breaks down the walls of the veins and arteries. But that's not what happened. He basically suffocated because of paralysis. He died from the effects of a neurotoxin, which works on the nerves. Some rattlesnakes have a lot of this kind of venom. But not the Eastern Diamondback."

"Do they know for sure which snake bit him? I understand Slaughter has a lot of them."

"Yes. They know. They got the right snake. Stu killed it and brought it with him when he drove Dobie down to meet the ambulance. They had the snake with them at the autopsy. The fang marks matched the wounds."

"Excuse me. That seems kind of screwy. They treated the snake like a murder weapon?"

"Maybe that's what it was. I hope not. But I want you to find out, if possible. What my caller suggested, and I find this horrifying, is that someone injected my husband with additional venom, to make sure he would die. I've been to Stu's little snake haven. He gave me the royal tour once. He milks his snakes and stores the venom in glass vials in a little refrigerator he keeps in the garage. When he gets enough, he takes it over to the college and sells it. He sells some to a vet too, who injects it into horses and makes antivenin from the blood. Poor horses.

"Stu keeps some of this antivenin on hand for emergencies. Only, it looks like it didn't work. He injected Dobie with some. He keeps a syringe in the little fridge too. So he could have injected my husband with extra venom. I really need to know.

"Dobie was pretty tight-lipped lately. But towards the end he opened up some. I know about some man pushing him into the lake. At first he told me he'd fallen in. And then he told me he thought Stu might have pushed him in. Dobie thought Stu and I might be having an affair. He was wrong. Do you know why he thought I was having an affair? Because I seemed so happy. That's really sad. And maybe it's my fault. I'm sad a lot. I can hardly leave the house. I'm almost a shut in. If it wasn't for my friend, Charlotte, I wouldn't get outside at all."

"Your husband told me you have agoraphobia. That's a tough break. Who's Charlotte? Does she live in Topaz Canyon?"

"Yes, she does. She has a brother and sister who run an optical shop."

My ears pricked up like a Doberman's. "I think I've met them. Is the brother named P.D. Slabov? Guy with a funny giggle?"

"That's right. How did you — ? You know, I'd feel a lot more comfortable if we could discuss all this face-to-face. Can you drive up?"

"I could if I had a car."

"I thought my husband loaned you a car."

"He did, but his sales manager, Spencer, repossessed it."

"Are you telling me Travis actually took the car away from you?"

"I figured you knew that."

"No. I wasn't informed. I own that car, and about a hundred others on Dobie's lots. Mr. Spencer needs a talking to. He didn't have my permission to collect that Nash from you. He just wants it for himself." Most of the satin and girlishness had left her voice. And the purr had turned into a growl. "Travis needs to get his comeuppance. I guess he thinks he can ride roughshod over the poor helpless widow. He probably believes he can take over the business. Listen, Mr. Hatchet, I promise you I'll get that car back to you. in less than an hour, or Mr. Spencer will be looking for a new job."

"Thanks, I appreciate it. I don't want to look a gift horse in the mouth, but, could you make it a different car this time? The Nash is a swell car, but it's not the kind of ride that suits a detective. There's a great old brown Chevy on your lot."

"No. I'm sorry, but it has to be that car. Travis wants it badly. He made a ridiculous offer to Dobie, and then got sore when Dobie laughed in his face. Travis took the car away from you so he could get his hands on it for himself. I'm sure of that. He needs to be taken down a peg, and that's how I'm going to do it."

"That's fine. It's a swell car. I'll be happy to take it."

"Will you also take the job I'm offering you?"

"It'll be my pleasure."

"I want a contract. Dobie told me he was paying you in chickens and pigs or something. That's not right. Dobie was a bit too frugal. So, if you could draw up a contract and bring it to me in Topaz Canyon, I'd appreciate it. I'll give you directions. I'd drop by your office but, as I told you, it's really hard for me to get out."

"No problem. I'd like a drive in the mountains. When would you like me to come up?"

"As soon as possible."

"I've been thinking. There's a friend of mine who knows a lot about snakes. He's not much for phone calls, so I'll have to drive over to talk to him. I would like to do that before I discuss the case any further with you."

"That's fine. Could you be here before noon?"

"I don't see why not. I'll see you in a couple of hours or so. And I'll bring a contract. Is there anything else I can bring you, since you're kind of housebound?"

"That's a kind offer, but, no. My friend Charlotte takes pretty good care of me."

"Her brother P.D. is an odd duck. Have you met

him?"

The line was silent for a moment, as if she was thinking about something.

"Yes. I've met him. He and his sisters are quite close. I think we should get off the phone now. I want to call Travis and arrange for the return of your car. The sooner I do that, the sooner you'll have it."

"All right. I'll see you later then."

We hung up.

While I waited for the Nash, I dusted off the typewriter and typed up a standard contract for Mrs. LeFever. It was nice to be working again, and not for free rent and car rental plus a little cash.

5

The widow was as good as her word. In no more than half-an-hour, I heard tires squeal in a quick stop outside. I ducked my head out the door. There was the Nash, with Spencer just emerging from the driver's seat. The second car was pretty showy too, and so was its driver. The car was a Lincoln convertible, Prussian blue, or some other kind of blue, and not too old. The driver who got out was a shapely miss, dressed like a secretary, and tossing around a lot of wavy blonde hair. I hurried down the steps.

"Here's your chariot, bub," Travis smiled at me, held out his bone crusher for me to shake. He was all affability today. The widow must have given him a good chewing.

"You even washed it for me."

"Nothing but the best for my little buddy. Axe, I want you to meet my secretary, Misty." He moved over to her and draped an ape-like arm around her shoulders. She was smiling, but there was a wince behind it. "Misty and me are getting hitched one of these bright days."

"What?" She pulled away from him, trying to make it look playful but not succeeding.

"Oh, I know you don't love me yet. But the day is coming, the day is coming." He fired off his laugh, scaring dogs within half-a-mile.

"Pleased to meet you, Misty. Try keeping this lad in line, will you?"

Misty said something, but I couldn't hear what because Travis treated the city to his laugh once more. As soon as I could, I got the keys to my car and sent the pair on their way.

I went up and locked my office door. I wasn't sure what Spencer had been up to with his flashy convertible and flashier dame, but I got the impression he was trying to save face somehow. It really didn't matter. I applied the key to the Nash and it took off like a tugboat. I was headed for the residence of Dr. Eben Mulford, and in less than twenty minutes I was there. It was a two-storied Victorian, painted peach, with plenty of cream-colored gingerbread.

As I climbed the steep stone steps that led to the front porch, I couldn't help feeling some trepidation. Don't get me wrong, I'm always happy to see my friend Mulford, but he really loves his snakes. I'm always expecting to step over half a dozen of them when I walk through his house.

I knocked on the big front door, which had an oval of etched glass. Two knocks. Then I pressed the door-bell three time. Then I repeated the two knocks. A secret signal known only to his friends. Forget trying to reach him on the phone. He owns one, but only uses it for making calls. He never answers the thing.

In a couple of minutes the front door creaked open. Retired professor of British literature, Eben Mulford, was at home. He looked his usual self. Short white hair and beard, reading glasses hanging from a chain around his neck, tiny body and eccentric clothes. He was the only person I knew, outside of Shriners, who wore a fez, and he only wore it at home. I'd talked to a couple of his old students, and was surprised to hear he'd been a rather dry, pedantic, professor.

"Axe, old man," he greeted me, though I was a good thirty-five years younger than him. "Come in, come in. I was just sitting down to a fascinating repast of sardines and toasted raisin bread. Will you join me?"

"No, thanks. But you can put on a pot of coffee."

I followed him through a living room cluttered with furniture. I thought I saw a white snake climbing up the wall, but it was only the pull cord for the drapes. We went down a little hall and ended up in an egg-yolk colored kitchen with a plentiful stock of cupboards. Eben fussed with coffee makings while I looked around. I was pretty sure I'd spotted a long black snake on the floor in a corner, but it was only an electrical cord.

I joined Eben in a lovely breakfast nook with a bay window pointed straight at the mountains. I drank coffee and watched him eat his mess of sardines and toast. We talked about this and that, and I finally got around to mentioning the reason for my visit.

"You still a fancier of the legless, cold- blooded, folk?"

"In happier circumstances," he said, interrupting his munching, "I would have made their study my life's work. Unfortunately, since my family financed my entire education, I bowed to their will and became a professor of English. However, I continued to study snakes on the side."

"So, you know something about snake poisons."

"Why? Did you come here to seek my expert advice? If so, I'll have to charge you." He frowned, looking suddenly petty and vicious. But I wasn't fooled.

"I've warned you, Eben. You keep playing the curmudgeon, someday your brain will freeze that way."

He laughed a snort of pure delight. "I do love the role. Now, how can I help you?"

"You read the papers? Did you read about that guy who died of snakebite? In Topaz Canyon. Got bit by a friend's great big Eastern Diamondback rattler."

Eben nodded. "An eight-footer. Too bad they had to kill it. The paper said he died on the way to the hospital. It's surprising he didn't die almost at once. People don't realize how potent rattlesnake venom is. Considerably more toxic than, say, cobra venom. But the cobra is a big snake, as well as being quite lovely."

"Yes, especially in the gloaming."

"It can inject several tablespoons of poison with just one bite. Rattlesnakes are generally much smaller."

"Yeah, the gloaming does nothing for them."

"But they are beautiful in full sunlight. They usually inject relatively small amounts of poison. An eight-foot rattler, on the other hand, is quite lethal. "

"I've been hired to investigate the circumstances of this poor guy's death. I have information — or, maybe it's misinformation — that there was something suspicious about his death. Maybe it wasn't an accident. LeFever may have died from the wrong kind of poison."

Eben cogitated. "Perhaps the Diamondback borrowed some other snake's poison. A friend's."

"Sure. LeFever suffocated. The venom paralyzed him. He died from the effects of a neurotoxin. Eastern Diamondbacks pack mostly hemotoxin."

"Thank you for that information, Axe. I'll add it to my small stock of knowledge."

"Happy to oblige. What do you think? Why did LeFever die from the wrong venom?"

"Well, there are many things to consider. You

haven't given me a lot of information. It's possible the unfortunate victim was simply more suscepti-ble to neurotoxins than most of us. Or, the snake could have been a hybrid, a cross between a Dia-mondback and some other kind of rattlesnake. A Mojave, for example. Of course, those two species don't live in the same part of the country. Perhaps their meeting was arranged through the post, like mail-order brides. We're seeing more hybrids these days, and there are some highly neurotoxic rattlesnakes that share territory with the Eastern Diamondback. However, since you're a detective, you probably prefer an explanation that involves foul play. You're such a grizzly character."

"Mom was a bear. Ask Dad."

"So, you and your informant would like to be-lieve that the snake's owner, or keeper, really — I don't believe snakes can be truly owned since they're such independent spirits — injected the stricken man with additional snake venom, want-ing to make sure he died. Of course, he hoped this would go undetected. This Stu Slaughter — what a gamey, violent, name! I went up to his place once, to see his pets. Quite a collection. I was envi-ous. He certainly has the apparatus for injecting poison into unsuspecting visitors. A refrigerator chock full of jars of venom."

"I heard they were vials."

"Vials, jars, quit interrupting. He has poison on hand. He has antivenin, and needles. He claims he gave LeFever a shot of antidote. Maybe he did. But he could have made a second injection of venom, using the same puncture mark. Or perhaps he put together a cocktail that combined antivenin and venom. In his haste he may have grabbed the wrong container of poison. He has a Mojave, and a Cascabel, and they're both highly neurotoxic.

"Let's say, Axe, for arguments sake — and to entertain you — that Slaughter, who had just milked some of his beauties, was chagrinned to realize that a man whom he apparently considered an enemy, had the bad luck of being bitten by a milked rattler. A veritable dud. So, he decides to take matters into his own hands. But this might have been his first murder. Perhaps he was nervous. He may have reached into the icebox to grab a vessel of Diamondback poison and accidently put his hand on a vial or jar containing the Mojave or Cascabel venom. What do you think?"

"You're the doctor. Sounds pretty possible to me. But how would I prove it? I guess the autopsy turned up some questions. Even so, if Slaughter did in fact murder LeFever, he may get away with it."

"More than likely, I'd say. Our world is not always a just one."

I finished my coffee and stood up to go. Eben was still working on his little snack. He's a slow eater, and our conversation had made him even slower.

"I can let myself out. Thanks for the information. I think you might have helped."

"Tell me, Axe, this little case of yours, does it involve a comely widow?"

"There's a widow. I can't say if she's a looker. She's reported to be, but I haven't actually met her. I'm on my way to her place right now. Why do you ask?"

"Because I know you're susceptible. Be careful. Rumor has it you're currently romantically involved with someone."

"Where'd you hear that?"

"I have my connections. Don't fall for the widow, Axe. You'll break your girl's heart. And I'm sure you've made her suffer enough already."

"I'll mind my P's and Q's, don't worry."

I left. I walked down the short hall and into the living room. I thought I saw a snake under a pie-crust lamp table. I took another step. It was a snake. I glued my feet to the floor. The snake rose up and spread its hood.

"Eben," I shouted, "Come get your damned cobra."

"Heavens," he shouted back, "it's only Evelyn. I had her venom sacks removed years ago. She's harmless. Give her a pat on the head and she'll stick her tongue out for you."

I declined that pleasure, stepped around the serpent, and skipped out to my car with more haste than dignity.

I thought Mulford's scenario of Slaughter's possible actions sounded reasonable. But how would I go about getting him to confess? Without his confessing, it wasn't likely he'd ever be charged — let alone convicted — for the murder. Mrs. LeFever knew Slaughter well. Maybe she could come up with some ideas about getting him to 'fess up. I hoped so.

6

I guided the Nash up the winding dirt road that led through Topaz Canyon. It was a nice enough drive. There was a sprinkling of rain, almost a mist, but not enough to affect the road. The widow had given me directions, and her house was easy to find. It was right next to the road. It was a two-storied log cabin, but not an old one. There were picture windows, a wrap-around porch on the second story, wooden shakes for shingles, and window boxes and ornamental shutters. A comfortable looking place.

I parked in a flat, wide, space, unpaved, directly off the road. There were steps to climb to the front door and I climbed them. There was no doorbell, just a big brass knocker. I used it. A moment later the door swung inward. A small woman peeked around the door.

"Mr. Hatchett?" I recognized the purr.

"Yes. Mrs. LeFever?"

"Come in. And call me Rolaine."

I stepped into a small foyer, though it was two-storied, and wiped my dusty feet on a rough matt left there for the purpose. I held my hat in my hand and looked into a living room that was also two-storied and featured multiple big windows.

"Call me Axe. Please."

"Come in and find a chair, Axe. Can I offer you anything? I have iced tea, Coke, or I can give you a real drink if it's not too early for you."

"Way too early. Nothing, thanks."

I found a seat on an ottoman that faced the couch that Rolaine had chosen for her seat. I had expected rustic furniture. You know, rocking chairs carved from tree stumps, couches made of big slabs of pine trees with the bark still on. Coffee tables fashioned from flat boulders. But everything was Danish modern, in blond wood, with tan and rust nubby upholstery. The only thing rustic in the room was the big native rock fireplace, with its mantle made from a split log.

As for Rolaine, there was nothing rustic about her, either. She was dressed like a high school girl. Cuffed jeans, saddle shoes, and a too-big man's white shirt. She didn't look much older than a high school girl either. She was short, fine boned, but still nicely curved. Her glossy black hair was worn in a thick braid down her back. I think it was a French braid, but it could have been Latvian for all I really knew. Her large eyes were black too, or at least as dark brown as eyes can be. Her mouth was wide, the lips full and red with lipstick. A long, straight nose and a small pointy chin completed the picture. Her beauty was of the kind that makes it hard not to stare.

"You have a nice house," I said, lamely.

"Thank you. Since I spend so much time here, I like it to be nice. Are you sure I can't get you anything? I know the drive up here can be a bit harrowing."

"I enjoyed it. Since you ask, if it's not too much trouble, I wouldn't mind a cup of coffee."

She smiled broadly, and rose gracefully from the couch.

"It'll only take a minute. I'll be in the kitchen if you need me."

She disappeared through an arched doorway and I was left to my own devices. I looked around the living room. Besides the furniture, there were some original oil paintings, mostly mountain scenes, and knick-knacks on the shelves of a built-in bookcase on one wall. Some of the knick-knacks were rock crystals. I wondered where Rolaine had gotten them.

In no more than ten minutes, Rolaine returned with a tray on which were a cup of coffee, with sugar bowl and cream pitcher, a glass of ice tea, and a plate of what looked like honest-to-God homemade oatmeal cookies.

"You didn't have to go to all that trouble."

"No trouble at all. I like entertaining. You can imagine, with my hardly getting out of the house, having people over is very important."

"Even private investigators?"

"Absolutely."

"Well, then, I hate to mix business with pleasure, but − " I pulled out the folded up contract from my inside coat pocket. I handed it to her. "Look that over, if you will. If you like it, I'll need your signature."

I think she read every damned word, frowning with concentration. Then she looked up and smiled. A couple of dimples showed that I hadn't noticed before.

"Do you have a pen?"

I pulled my fountain pen from the same inside pocket and handed it to her. I've never made peace with ball points. The ones I used during the war seemed to be filled with colored oil instead of ink. She added her autograph to the bottom of the contract, fanned it a couple of times to dry the ink, and gave it back to me.

"I hope you can help me. I so need to know if Stu murdered Dobie."

"I'll try to help you, but it's going to be tough. I'll likely need to talk Slaughter into confessing. Or trick him into confessing. The friend I just talked to, the snake expert, says the notion of Slaughter's injecting your husband with extra venom seems plausible."

"I hope it's not true. But if it is, Stu has to pay for the crime. That's all there is to it."

"You've known him a long time. Any ideas about how I can get him to talk? I thought I'd drop by his place today, since I'm in the neighborhood. You'll need to give me directions. Do you suppose he's home?"

"It's likely. It's too early in the year for him to be out guiding hunters. I can give you directions. We own the place, you know. I own the place. As for getting him to talk, that might prove difficult. Stu's not much of a talker. And he's stubborn. You'll have to be careful how you approach him. Don't let him know you're a detective, or that you're working for me. Just talk to him for a while, then gradually lead up to the subject of the snake-bite accident."

"Sounds like sound advice. Maybe I should get headed over there now. No time like the present."

"He'll likely be home most of the day. Finish your coffee and cookies, and then I have a favor to ask."

"A favor?"

"Nothing too difficult. For you. It'll be difficult for me. I was wondering if you'd take a walk in the garden with me. We call it a garden, but actually it's just a clearing in the woods out back. A little stream runs through it."

"Sounds lovely. Of course I'll tour the garden with you."

I chomped on a couple of more cookies, washed them down with coffee, and I stood up, ready to go.

"Dobie's funeral is Monday. I hope I'll be able to go. The cemetery is so big and open. We had a small memorial service here, this morning. Well, I'm ready. Let's go."

She led me through a long galley kitchen and into a small mudroom beyond. Then we went out the back door and down a flight of wooden steps. As soon as we'd stepped outdoors, Rolaine had clutched my upper arm with both her delicate hands. We slowly walked around the clearing. The stream made a pleasant sound of rippling as it passed over the rocky bed. There was a swing with an awning, a couple of lawn chairs, and a birdbath presently devoid of birds. Rolaine's hands trembled on my arm. Her voice, when she spoke, was a fierce whisper, and her eyes looked almost wild. For being as small as she was, she put out a lot of heat.

"I wasn't always this way," she told me. "I remember being afraid of the outdoors as a young child. But I was afraid of everything then. I got over it. I used to ride around behind Stu, on his motorcycle. I loved it. My agoraphobia didn't start again until after my marriage. On our honeymoon, actually.

"Dobie had bought a used Cadillac. He was just getting started back then. He was still a salesman. The Cadillac had a powerful motor. Dobie was very proud of the car. We spent two weeks driving all over Colorado. We traveled over many mountain passes. Some of the mountains were so far above sea level that there was hardly any vegetation. Short grass. Stunted trees. Nothing else but low piles of rocks. I began to get afraid. You could see for miles from those bare peaks, with nothing to block the view. I had a breakdown of some sort. We had to cut our honeymoon short. Dobie was very kind, at first.

"The saddest part of all was that we couldn't have children. Dobie wanted them so badly. Girls to spoil. Boys to teach baseball, and to take over the business someday. But I didn't want our children to have a mother who could hardly leave the house. We put off having a family. Dobie didn't believe in head doctors, as he called them. I went to regular doctors. They gave me tranquilizers and told me to spend more time outdoors. I tried, I really did.

"Dobie should have left me, found some other woman to have children with, but he didn't believe in divorce. He thought it was failure. I would have left him myself, given him his freedom, but how could I when I could scarcely go outdoors?

"After a time he started having affairs. Short, meaningless, encounters. He hardly bothered to hide what he was doing. And he paid less and less attention to me. I was so lonely. He would bring home his men friends. Salesmen mostly. Some of them were attracted to me, and I let them sleep with me. But it only made me more lonely." She looked up at the sky and shivered. "I don't know why I'm telling you all this. It's very selfish of me."

"It's my face. Women and dogs can't leave me

alone. If it makes you feel any better, go ahead and talk. It won't go any farther. I promise."

"Thank you. I thought things might get better when Stu got back from Africa. I practically threw myself at him. But he kept his distance. I wasn't the girl he remembered, the one who loved riding with him on his motorcycle. I was broken. More broken than he was with his injured back. Then things got better for me. I met my friends, Charlotte and Ann. They've been very kind, especially Charlotte. She's helped. She's made me feel braver, less alone. And then I met someone else. A man. We became lovers."

"Can I ask you the guy's name? Anyone I know?"

She shook her head. "You can have my secrets, but not someone else's. Dobie knew something was going on. He thought Stu and I had finally gotten together. And I let him believe that, to protect my true lover. Then, as you know, someone tried to drown Dobie. I hope it wasn't Stu. It would make no sense. Even revenge for the loss of his eye wouldn't make sense after all these years. I know Dobie'd been treating Stu badly lately. Maybe Stu had had enough of him."

"Let's just hope the snakebite was really an accident. I'm not sure I trust your college-boy informant. He might be a crank. Anyway, I'll do what I can to get to the bottom of things. Oh, by the way, thanks for the use of the car."

"You need a car until you get yours back. Besides, I love the idea of dangling that lovely car over Travis Spencer's head. He needs to learn his new boss isn't a pushover. You, know, Travis tried to make love to me, behind Dobie's back. He's a disgusting person. As soon as I can find a replacement for him, I'll have Travis fired.

"I want to go in now, please. Thank you for walking with me, and for listening to my sordid story. Don't think too badly of me."

"Not a chance. You should hear my story. Let me help you inside."

7

Once we were back in the house, Rolaine gave me directions to Slaughter's. She said it was no more than a couple of miles from her own place. I took my time driving to Slaughter's house. I wanted time to think about what I was going to say to him. I didn't want him to put his guard up. I found the address. It was a low, rambling, frame building with an attached two-car garage. Pretty nice, although it looked like it would need painting in the near future.

I walked to the front door and knocked. There was no answer. I knocked again, harder. I had just stepped off the porch with the idea of going around to the back of the house, when the neighbor lady from across the road called out to me.

"He's not home. He's walking his dog. He'll likely be back in a few minutes. Come talk to me while you're waiting."

I crossed the road. The woman was maybe in her late twenties, early thirties, long boned and almost too thin. Her dull black hair was clearly dyed. She had lavender eyes and freckles.

"Are you Charlotte?"

She gave me a quizzical smile. "How do you know me?"

"I've met your friend, Rolaine. She spoke to me of your kindness. She says you've helped her a lot."

The smile became blinding, and as long as it lasted, she was beautiful.

"Why do you want to see my friend, Stu? Is it about the snakebite business?"

"Yes. Just routine questions." I dug in my wallet and pulled out somebody else's card. It said my name was Preston Mitten, and that I was an insurance investigator. "Nothing to worry about. My company insures Mr. Slaughter's home. When something like this happens, well, let's just say it generates a lot of paperwork."

"Why don't you talk to me about the accident? I was practically a witness!"

"I didn't know there had been any witnesses besides Mr. Slaughter. I don't think the papers mentioned you."

"That's Stu's doing. He's trying to protect me, keep the police and the press from bothering me. But I was here when it happened. I was sitting on my front porch, just like today, reading through a batch of children's books to see if they'll fit our collection. I'm a librarian, did you know that?"

"Mrs. LeFever mentioned it to me."

"I saw Mr. LeFever drive up in his truck. I'd met him a couple of times when he'd come to Stu's house to talk to him. I shouted hello, but I don't think he heard me. At the time I thought he was snubbing me, so when he knocked on Stu's door I didn't tell him Stu wasn't home. Let the guy knock, I thought."

"Where was Mr. Slaughter?"

"Walking his dog, just like today. Ernie needs a lot of exercise."

"Ernie? The dog?"

"Yes. Anyway, after Mr. LeFever had knocked a couple of times, he took a key from his pocket and let himself in. I guess that's his right as a land-lord."

"Not under those circumstances."

"He was in the house for several minutes, enough time for Stu to return from his walk. Stu recognized the car and figured out what was going on. I walked down the road to meet him. That's when we heard the screaming. It sounded like it was coming from Stu's garage, and it was horrible. We got to the house as soon as we could and went inside. I chained Ernie to the front porch while Stu went on inside.

"Stu was already in the garage when I joined him. Mr. LeFever was lying on the floor, and he looked awful. His face was as red as your car, and he was gasping for breath. On the floor near him was the snake. Dead. Stu had grabbed a hammer off his workbench and thrown it at the rattler. It crushed its head. Stu told me to go call the hospital, so I ran back into the house and used the phone in the living room. When I returned to the garage, Stu was just giving Mr. LeFever a shot of antivenin. Do you know what that is?"

"Yeah."

"I told Stu and Mr. LeFever that an ambulance was on the way, then Stu got the idea of helping Mr. LeFever into his truck and driving down to meet the ambulance. We got the poor man out to the truck. I wanted to go along, but Stu wouldn't let me. When Stu gets an idea in his head, nobody can talk him out of it."

"I see. And how was the victim, when you were loading him into the truck?"

"Bad. His face had gone from red to blue, and he seemed out of his head. When I found out later that he'd died, I wasn't surprised. Look, there's Stu."

I looked in the direction she was looking. About twenty yards down the road a man and his dog were approaching. The man was tall, and very thin, but wide in the shoulders. Cords of muscle showed in the arms that emerged from his short-sleeved shirt. He had a light, careful, walk, as if he thought he was treading on fresh éclairs.

The dog was a monster. It looked like something Slaughter might have brought home from Africa with him. Half crocodile, half hippo. When Slaughter saw me, he stopped, reached down, and clipped a leash to Ernie's spiked collar. Then he resumed walking.

"I'll leave the two of you alone," Charlotte said. "Nice talking to you, Mr. Mitten. I hope everything works out for Stu. It really was just an accident, and I don't see how Stu can be blamed."

"Like I said, I only have some routine questions. Nice meeting you."

I headed up the road to meet the couple, though I wasn't too sure I wanted to make Ernie's acquaintance. The closer I got to Slaughter, the more the dog growled. When there was no more than twenty feet separating us, the man told me to halt. His voice was quiet, but it carried. I could see his face well now. It was sun-darkened, and there were networks of wrinkles around his eyes and along his forehead. Aside from that, he seemed a handsome fellow, in a hard-bitten kind of way. I could imagine a certain sort of woman falling for him. He was wearing sunglasses, the lenses dark enough that I could see nothing of his eyes.

"Can I help you?" he asked, in his quiet, level voice.

"I'd hand you my card, but I doubt your dog will let me."

To my surprise, he kneeled down by Ernie and appeared to whisper in the dog's ear. Whatever he said, it had the desired effect. He resumed walking toward me and, though the dog kept his yellow eyes on me, he was no longer growling. We slowly walked towards each other like a couple of old time gunfighters. When we were close enough,

I handed him Mitten's card. He read it with care.

"You related to Dexter Mitten?"

"No. Sorry, I never heard of him. Friend of yours?"

"He was. He got eaten alive by a pack of hyenas, or so I heard. How can I help you? Is this about the snake accident?"

"Yes, in a way."

"I've already talked to the cops. Twice. And some folks at the hospital. And from the newspaper. I even got a call from a coroner. I'm kind of tired of the subject, but I guess that's how things are going to be for me for a while."

"Sorry. I'll try not to use up more of your time than necessary. I've already spoken to Miss — ?" I gestured over my shoulder at Charlotte's house.

"Mews. Charlotte Mews. I tried to keep her out of it, but she's as stubborn as me. I've got a suggestion. Why don't I take you into my garage and we can recreate the accident." He must have noticed the startled look on my face. "Only up to a certain point of course." He smiled, which made his wrinkles fan out all over .his face. His teeth were straight and strong looking, but yellow. "Come on inside. I'll chain Ernie up."

"I appreciate your cooperation."

We walked together to his front door. He chained poor Ernie to the porch and we went inside. We were in a smallish living room dominated by a white quartz fireplace. Above the fireplace hung the biggest rifle I'd ever seen. I gestured toward it, and Slaughter smiled again. He took off his sunglasses, and I couldn't help but notice his eyes. The left eyelid drooped a little but the glass eye was a perfect match for the real one. Both were a glittering gray-blue.

"That's a four-seventy Holland and Holland double barreled big game rifle," he said "There's not an animal on earth that rifle can't bring down. I ought to know, I've used it to shoot most kinds."

We passed through the living room, getting a peek at the kitchen through an arched double doorway. Then we entered a small room that might have been intended as a spare bedroom. The walls were decorated with spectacular African animal heads. There was a Cape buffalo, a lion, a leopard, a gorilla, even a rhinoceros. The heads crowded the room so badly I felt I was under siege by wild animals.

"Impressive, aren't they?" Slaughter said. "When I finally left Africa, I brought them with me, but I had to leave others behind, including a splendid bull elephant with six-foot-long tusks."

I was glad when we left this room, crossed a dark hall, and entered the garage. But I wasn't glad for very long. The garage was only dimly lit, and our entrance was greeted by the rattling of at least twenty snakes.

"This is where it happened."

"I don't suppose you could turn some lights on."

"Sure. I keep it dim because the snakes like it

that way." He switched on some overhead florescent lights. I could see the wire-screened cages now, and many of their inmates. Some snakes had roommates, while others were in solitary. Showing a bravado I really didn't feel, I made a tour of the room, with Slaughter closely following me.

"What's up with this one? He looks like a baby."

"Nope. He's full grown. That's a Faded Midget."

"And this guy over here? Did his rattles fall off?"

"That's a Santa Catalina Island rattler. They're only found on one island. They don't grow rattles. They just have that nub on the end of their tails. They can't warn you before they strike."

"I'll keep that in mind. So, where exactly did the accident take place?"

He led me to a spot a few yards away.

"Here. This is where I found Dobie. He was lying down on the floor, screaming. The Diamondback was here." He pointed to a spot a few feet from where LeFever had been. There was a spattering of blood on the concrete floor.

"You killed the snake?"

"With a hammer. I threw it at him. It was a lucky throw. I hit it in the head."

"So, the snake was loose when Mr. LeFever entered the garage."

"I guess. I can't imagine Dobie opening its cage. They get out sometimes. They nose open the latches somehow. That's why I don't take people into my garage that often. That's why I lock up my house when I'm gone. Dobie had a key. He had no legal right to enter my house when I was gone — I don't care if he was the landlord. Surely that's a violation of tenant rights?"

"I think 'tenant rights' is an oxymoron in Quartz Quarry."

"Topaz Canyon isn't officially part of the city. We're considered our own special rural area. That's why I'm able to keep all these rattlers. In Topaz Canyon you could keep a pet mountain lion if you wanted to. Believe me, I've checked."

"OK. So Mr. LeFever violated your tenant rights when he unlocked your door and came into your house. Maybe he looked around a little. Any reason why he'd do that?"

"You mean because he thought I was dealing drugs or something? I can't imagine he thought any such thing. We knew each other a long time. Since grade school."

"So, maybe he wanted to check on the snakes for some reason of his own. He goes into the garage. There's a snake loose. It bites him. He screams. According to Miss Mews, you and she hurried into the house to see what was going on."

"That's right, though I wish you'd keep her out of it. We found Dobie. I sent Charlotte to phone for an ambulance. I killed the snake, then checked on Dobie. He'd been struck on the leg. I applied a tourniquet above the wound, and then I gave him a shot of antivenin. He shouldn't have died.'

"Where do you keep this antivenin?"

"In that fridge." He pointed to a little icebox in one corner.

"I understand you milk these snakes and sell their venom."

"That's correct. It helps me make ends meet in the slow seasons. I'm a hunting guide."

"Do you keep the venom in that same fridge with the antivenin?"

"I do. Why not?"

"No reason. You said you talked to our coroner. Did he tell you about the autopsy the medical examiner performed?"

"He told me something about it. He said there was something screwy about it."

"Did he give details?"

"No. I didn't ask. Why should I care if the autopsy was screwy? I know what happened that day."

"Apparently there was some kind of confusion about what sort of poison killed Mr. LeFever. Listen, this is just an idea. When you gave him the antivenin, you must have been pretty flustered."

"Not me. Mister, have you ever gone into the African bush, by yourself, to finish off a wounded leopard?"

"Not that I recall."

"I've done it. One of the most dangerous things I've ever done. Leopards are smart. They'll wait for you. They can be dying, and they'll find a way to kill you before they die. If I wasn't flustered then, and I wasn't, why would I be flustered just because I was giving somebody a shot?"

"I'm just trying to figure things out. Maybe when you went to grab the container of antivenin you accidentally got hold of a bottle of snake poison instead. You might have innocently given your friend an injection of poison. Is that just barely possible?"

"No. I'll show you."

He took me over to the fridge and opened it. It was about a quarter full of glass containers. He grabbed one and held it up.

"You see this? It's a beaker. When you're ready to milk a snake, you take one of these beakers and you stretch a thin rubber cover over it. Then you grab the snake, right behind the head, and squeeze. It'll usually open its mouth. Then you force it to puncture the rubber lid with its fangs. It will generally squirt its venom right into the beaker. You pull the rubber cover and throw it away. Then you replace it with one of these thicker rubber lids."

He showed me one. Then he reached back into the fridge and brought out a slender vial, with a little rubber and metal cap.

"This is the antivenin. Now, tell me, how flustered would you have to be to mistake one of those beakers for one of these vials? It couldn't happen."

"Listen, Mr. Slaughter, I'm just trying to do my

job. I've got reports to fill out. I'm trying to find out what might have happened. I'm not accusing you of anything, And I didn't come here with any preconceived notions about what happened that tragic day."

He gave me a glare an elephant wouldn't have liked. Then his shoulders sagged a little and he smiled.

"You're right, pal. Is it Milton?"

"Mitten."

"You deal in home owners insurance?"

"Yeah, I know. It doesn't sound like it makes much sense, does it? But I didn't realize — my company didn't realize — that you could keep exotic pets in Topaz Canyon. That was the sticking point. Now it looks like I've just wasted your time."

"That's all right. I still owe you an apology. I shouldn't have gotten mad at you. Can I offer you something? A drink? I've got a pretty good bottle of gin, and I make a mean martini. I used to make them on safari. After a long day of hunting in the African savannas, there's nothing like an ice cold dry martini."

"You're tempting me, but I'm still on the clock. Thanks, anyway. And thank you for your time and your cooperation."

He showed me out. We passed through the dim hall again, across the trophy room, and back into the living room.

"If I was going to murder somebody," he said,

pointing at the rifle above the fireplace, "that's how I'd do it."

"Harder to get by with."

"It can be arranged."

He showed me to the door. Charlotte was standing beside the porch, talking to Ernie and scrubbing his ears while he wagged his tail and slobbered all over her.

"Nice to have met you, Miss Mews," I told her. "You too, Ernie."

Ernie growled. I walked to my car and got in. I took one last look at the trio by the porch. Slaughter and Charlotte were standing close and smiling. I wondered if Slaughter felt the same way about the librarian as Ernie did. Just an idle thought.

8

On the drive back to Quartz Quarry proper, I thought about Charlotte, and I thought about Slaughter. The man hadn't been exactly cordial, but he'd been forthcoming enough. And when I'd given him the opportunity to cop the plea that he may have accidentally injected LeFever with poison, he had shot down the idea immediately. He had practically proven that such an accident could not have happened.

Did that mean he was innocent? Could be. I really hadn't come away from the Slaughter abode with any information that would help prove, or disprove, that he'd murdered his old friend and rival. That left me nowhere. Wouldn't Rolaine be tickled pink that her detective had accomplished nothing? But that's the way it goes sometimes.

As for Charlotte, had she really been a witness of Dobie's dilemma? Or was she trying to cover for Stu, whether he wanted her to or not? Were they lovers? Did Rolaine know? Would it matter to her? When it comes to affairs of the heart, you often end up with a great big mess. Such is love, and all that goes with it.

I was beginning to think I might want to return to Topaz Canyon in the morning. Tomorrow was Sunday. I hoped I could at least find Charlotte or Stu at home. I'd gently hammer away until someone said something that they wished they hadn't said. Beyond that, I really had no plan

Because of my recent lack of wheels, and Tracy's lack of a car, I hadn't seen her for three days. Since I was getting hungry anyway, I headed for Rocko's Or, should I call it Cookie's? Or, Calvin's? When I parked in front of the diner and went inside, I found my little Cabbage Roll in attendance as usual, brightening the life of a vacuum cleaner salesman who had stopped in for a grilled cheese sandwich.

"You don't like the cheese we use?" Tracy was shouting at the poor guy. "How would you like blue cheese, or cottage cheese? We use good American cheese for our grilled cheese sandwiches. What are you, some kind of pinko?"

The guy gulped down the remainder of his meal, paid the tab, and hurried out of the place without saying goodbye.

Tracy turned to me. "What do you want, stranger? I recommend the meat loaf."

"You've been pushing that meat loaf for months now."

"Somebody's got to eat it, and it's not going to

be me. So, you got the red bus back?" She gestured at the Nash outside the window. "You've got to buy it, you know. It keeps following you home."

"You know, if I thought I could trade the Hornet for the Ambassador, straight across, I might just do it. The Hudson's a year older, but it cost more new. Is Cookie up to burning a couple of egg sandwiches, with onion, and some of your wonderful American cheese? Maybe some grease-drowned fries on the side?"

"I don't know. I'll ask. I think he's doing his nails." She hollered my order through the hole in the wall behind her, and Cookie gave an answering howl. Tracy poured me a cup of coffee, leaving a puddle for whatever thirsty roaches might be around.

"So, you must be working again. Since you have that car, you must be working for that LeFever dame"

"She's a lady, not a dame."

"Oh, I see. Good looking, huh? Curves like a roller coaster, a whole lot of fluffy hair, big bedroom eyes? All the good stuff."

"She's OK to look at. You've got nothing to worry about."

"Oh, I wasn't worrying. Who, besides me, would submit to being your girl?"

"That's what I mean. That's what I just said. I'm back working again, but don't start spending my money yet."

"Hey, I'm still busy spending my own. You know, I've been thinking."

"Don't do that. Stick to wiping down counters with wet diapers."

"Look, just because I said 'yes' the first time you asked me out, that doesn't mean I don't have brains, though it's pretty good evidence. I've been thinking about the tip money I've been saving all this time. I was saving it for surgery to make myself taller, but now I've got a better idea. I want a car. Can I get a decent car for three-hundred smackers?"

"You serious about wanting a car? Sure, you could get a nice enough used jalopy for that kind of money. Why the sudden urge to own wheels? You're a home body."

"I might want to go places someday. Or maybe I'll take up stock car racing."

"Tie one of your counter rags to your bumper and none of the other stock cars will dare pass you."

Our billing and cooing was interrupted by the arrival of my food. I ate in silence while I gave Tracy a good looking over. I decided she was more compact than short. And the eyes I'd once called mud-brown were actually more like fawn eyes. They were squinty, but that's because she refused to wear her glasses. Her teeth were over-sized, which made for a good smile on the rare occasions she was inclined to share it. Her figure was a bit overblown, but you want a girl to look like a girl, don't you? Now her hair, it was fuzzier than the classical ideal, but it was softer than a Brillo pad. As to her nose, it didn't quite go with the rest of her. It was perfect. Small, upturned, freckled, with nostrils of equal size. What a swell lady.

"If this case goes the way I'm hoping," I told her, "you and me are going out someplace swell."

"The carnival?"

"Is that what you want?"

"I love shooting BBs at little tin animals. And hitting those little wooden milk bottles with baseballs. I'm good at it. I've got a closet full of kewpies. And the food. And the fortune tellers. They're always wrong. I don't know how they do it!"

"OK, then. Carnival here we come!"

I was up and out early the next morning. It had rained in the night in Topaz Canyon, and the road was thick with slippery mud, but the bright sun was already drying things out. When I drove past Rolaine's I thought of stopping, but it might be better to talk to her later, after I'd found out something that mattered.

I drove on up to within a quarter-of-a-mile of Charlotte's and Stu's, then I pulled off the road and switched off the engine. I needed time to think. I hadn't really planned out what I was going to say, or to whom I was going to say it. I got out of the car and paced up and down and looked around. I couldn't see even one house. That's how isolated this part of Topaz Canyon is. I fired up a cigar. That often helps me in my ruminating.

I was about halfway through the cigar, and was about to go take the tiger by the tail, when a gunshot rang out and echoed through the canyon. A rifle shot. It was too low-pitched to be from a handgun. My gut told me the shot was bad news for someone. It had come, as near as I could tell, from up the road a ways, from the direction of Stu's and Charlotte's houses.

I don't know why I took off running instead of getting back in the car, but that's what I did. I clamped my cigar between my teeth and took off for where I'd heard the shot as fast as a short-legged thirty-six year can go. Before I could round the corner that would put me in sight of Charlotte's and Stu's houses, I heard the frantic barking of a dog. It had to be Slaughter's mutt.

At first I didn't see the body. He was lying on his back near the front porch that Ernie was chained to. There was blood high up on his shirt, but not much. I feared the bullet had struck his heart and stopped it. The body didn't so much as twitch, and the limbs were splayed out like a drunken scarecrow's. I tried to get closer, but the dog was having none of it. I needed to find a phone. I thought I'd try Slaughter's back door, but I remembered what he'd said the day before about keeping his place locked up. That left Charlotte's.

My breath was coming fast, but I sprinted across the road and up onto her porch. The door was locked. I ran around to the back. That door was locked as well. What was wrong with these country folk? They're supposed to be friendly and trusting! I used a trick I'd learned from a locksmith client of mine; I took a couple of lock picks from my wallet and went to work. In a couple of minutes I had the door open.

I entered the kitchen, and the phone was on the wall. I used it. I called for an ambulance, then I grabbed the phone book that was on the counter and looked up the number for the Quartz Quarry Public Library. I didn't know if they were even open on Sundays, but it was worth a try. I got lucky — somebody answered. I asked to speak to the children's librarian, and in couple of minutes I was talking to Charlotte.

"Listen, it's me, Axe Hatchett. We met yesterday at your place. I was using a different name. I'd like to be more sensitive about this, but I'm in an awful hurry. Something's happened to your friend, Stu. He's been shot. I'm afraid he's dead."

There was a gasp on the other end of the line, but she didn't say a word.

"I've called for an ambulance. I haven't called the cops yet, and I hope the hospital didn't. I need you to get here as fast as you can. Ernie won't let me get anywhere near the body. I'm sure he'll give the cops the same greeting. Look, they might shoot the dog. You might be the only one who can keep that from happening. The mutt likes you."

"Oh, my God. I can't believe this. Stu, shot.

Dead. I'm on my way. I'll speed to get there. Don't let them hurt Ernie."

We hung up and I called the cops. I got a dispatcher and gave him the news, then I gave him some pretty vague directions to Stu's house. I just couldn't think clearly. I went out the back door, and that's when I noticed a couple of things I hadn't noticed coming in. Most of the mud from yesterday's rain had dried up, but there was a little shady spot near the back porch that showed two clear footprints. They weren't Charlotte's. They had been made by a man's work boots, and they were leading away from the little crawlspace door next to the back steps. Near them was a beautiful greenish-blue crystal. It looked like turquoise, but I didn't think turquoise formed in crystals.

I should have left the stone alone, but I'm always doing things I shouldn't do. Especially when cops are involved. I picked up the crystal and put it in my pocket, then I skirted the footprints and went around to the front of the house. I looked under the front porch. There was a gap between the first and second step. The sniper could have used the rear crawlspace door, slithered under the house, and ended up peeping through the gap in the front porch steps. It would have given him a swell view of Slaughter's front yard, and the sniper would have been practically invisible.

My cigar was still clamped between my teeth, so I puffed on it. I sat on the front steps and wait-

ed for the parade to show up. The ambulance arrived first. It's siren was off. The ambulance crew
consisted of the driver and two attendants. They
dragged a stretcher out of the back but Ernie
wouldn't let any of us get near the body. We stood
around smoking and waiting for the next member
of the party to arrive.

I hoped it would be Charlotte. It wasn't. Two
cop cars showed up. One a black-and-white, with
its siren blaring stupidly, and the other a gray
unmarked job. Two beefy, uniformed officers got
out of the black and white. A short guy in a too-
large tan fedora got out of the other car. They all
stood around glaring at us and asking us too
many questions.

"He's dead," I volunteered. "The dog won't let
anybody near him."

Tan Hat took a plain-end cigarette out of his
mouth, spat out some shreds of tobacco, and
turned to the bigger of the uniformed cops.

"Flanders," he said. "Shoot that damned dog"

Flanders unlimbered his service revolver, licked
his lips, and took careful aim. I got between him
and the dog.

"You don't have to do that," I said. "The neighbor lady's on her way, probably breaking some
speeding laws. She should be here any minute.
She can handle the dog. They're friends."

"Step aside, Buster," Flanders told me. "This is
police business. Get out of the way or I'll put a pill
in your puss."

This was too much for Tan Hat.

"Flanders, put the gun up. The guy's right. That stiff's not going anywhere. We can spare a couple of minutes for the lady to show up."

With obvious reluctance, Dead-Eye Flanders holstered his piece. I heard a car approaching, but it wasn't Charlotte's cute little yellow Jeepster. It was a dark green Dodge. Probably the coroner, I thought, and I was right. He got out of the Dodge and fired up a briar pipe. The eight of us stood around smoking and waiting for the winsome librarian. Finally, she showed.

"Flat tire?" I asked her.

"No. Lousy traffic." She looked at all of us, saw that I was standing between Ernie and Annie Oakley. She gave me a grateful look.

"I can handle the dog," she told all of us. "He's really quite obedient. I'll take him into my house." She hurried over to Ernie, unsnapped the chain from his collar, and guided him across the road and into her house. If she'd looked at the body even once, I didn't see her do it. In less than a minute she was back across the road and standing next to me. She wasn't smoking.

The ambulance crew went about confirming what they doubtless already suspected. Slaughter was dead, shot once in the chest. Then the three men backed away and let the cops and the coroner swarm all over the scene. They squinted at the ground, they took pictures, and they wrote things in notebooks. The coroner puffed his pipe and kept looking at his watch. Finally, he drove away, probably to some nice Sunday dinner.

When the cops were through snooping around, they gave the ambulance crew the go-ahead to haul off the body, probably to the morgue. When the ambulance drove off, slow as a hearse, Tan Hat came over and talked to me and Charlotte. Mostly to me.

"You're a private dick, aren't you? I've seen you around."

"That's right." I got out a card and showed him.

"I suppose it's only a coincidence, your being here at the scene of an apparent homicide. Just taking a nice Sunday drive, right?"

"Exactly. Enjoying nature. I saw a flock of humming birds. And a flower."

"Did you know this guy?" He jerked a thumb in the direction of the body, though it wasn't there anymore.

"I talked to him yesterday. About that snake business. I've been hired to look into the matter."

"That so? Who hired you?"

"My client."

"And who's your client, damn you?"

"The person who hired me to investigate the snake incident. That's why I'm here today. I was going to ask him some more questions."

"What questions?"

"Private eye stuff. Quit riding me. I had nothing to do with the shooting, and I don't have information that would help you solve the case."

He gave me a sour look, shook a Paul Mall out of a crumpled package, and used at kitchen match to light it. He took a couple of puffs, then spat out shreds of tobacco.

"You might want to switch to the filtered kind."

"Naw. I ain't no pansy. Where'd you get the phone to call us?"

I jerked a thumb of my own at Charlotte's house.

"How'd you get in?"

"The door was unlocked. You know these country folk. They're so friendly and trusting."

"How'd you know where to call this lady? And how'd you know she could handle the dog?"

"I met her yesterday, when I came up to talk to Slaughter. I saw her with the dog. He liked her. She told me she worked at the public library. So, I called there hoping she'd be there."

He turned to Charlotte. "How well did you know this guy? The stiff?"

"He was my neighbor. My friend. I have no idea why anyone would want to kill him."

Tan Hat grunted. "We might want to talk to you again. Don't leave town. If you've got plans to fly to Hawaii, cancel them. You can go for now. We'll be over when we're through looking around here to check out your yard. Maybe your house."

He turned back to me. "You can go too, peeper. Keep your nose clean. No more nature drives. At least, not if they take you out of town."

"I've got no such plans."

9

Charlotte was already crossing the road. I caught up with her. We went up on her front porch.

"I can't invite you in. Ernie."

"That's all right. I just wanted to ask you a favor. "

Tan Hat yelled at me from Stu's yard. "That your red ocean liner down the road?"

"Yeah."

"You said you came here when you heard a shot. Why'd you ditch the car?"

"I'm not sure, exactly. I panicked. I was taking a little nature walk when I heard the shot. I just took off running."

He nodded, turned his back to me, and started talking again with the uniformed cops.

"Listen," I told Charlotte. "When I was breaking into your house to use the phone, I noticed a couple of footprints next to your porch. Boot prints. I'm guessing they belong to the shooter. I'd like to see if I can follow his trail before all these flatfoots start stomping around. However, I don't want them catching me at it. Any way you can warn me if they come over here before I get a good start on them?"

"I'll have Ernie bark. He knows tricks."

"Thanks. Listen, I'm really sorry about Slaughter."

"Thanks. And thanks for standing up for the dog, too. I guess he'll be mine now."

I made a big show of walking into the road and heading back to my car. I even waved at Tan Hat. But as soon as I was out of sight, I crossed over into the woods and worked my way around to Charlotte's backyard.

I found the boot prints again, and did my best to find more of them. It was tough tracking. I didn't find any more mud. I had to look for displaced rocks, broken sticks, scuffed patches of pine needles. But I didn't lose the trail. I felt pretty proud of myself. I learned my tracking skills from my part-time operative, Bram Duckers. He claims to be part Indian. To me he looks about as Indian as Maimie Van Doren, but what do I know?

The tracks led through the woods to an old miner's cabin that was scarcely more than a pile of rotting logs. Behind the ruined cabin was a natural depression several feet deep. It had apparently been used as a trash dump, by the miner, for many years, and was half filled with rusted tin cans and as many bottles as had escaped the. bottle collectors. I looked this heap over pretty carefully, without touching anything. I decided it looked like it had been disturbed recently. Perhaps very recently. I walked around the area a little more and came across what looked like fresh truck tire tracks. Then I retraced my steps and crept through the woods to my car.

Between the hike, and the run I'd had earlier, I was beat. I was glad to slide behind the wheel of the Nash and head home. As I passed by Rolaine's house, I thought of stopping and giving her the sad news, but I decided I wasn't the person to tell her. No doubt her friend Charlotte would inform her of what had happened. I had other fish to fry. I had a cop to bribe. My next door neighbor.

Officer Blythe Bliss hailed from west Texas, and she'd been part of the Quartz Quarry Police Department for only a few months. Blythe was an energetic fireplug of a woman, a bit broad in the beam, with a lot of curly hair and the face of a jilted angel. She'd been living next door to me for three months. Just when you think you've settled into a decent neighborhood, the cops move in and the property values start going down.

Blythe was OK though. She was as noisy and over-friendly as most folks from her part of the world, but after she'd attempted to borrow multiple cups of sugar from me — I never buy sugar — I drink my coffee black, and most of my cooking consists of bacon and eggs and an occasional trout — she gave up pestering me. But now I needed her as my friend. I was yearning for some inside information, and she could give it to me. Hence the bribe I intended to generously offer her.

Officer Bliss rode a desk down at the local P.D., but I knew she had aspirations to drive a cruiser. I could never imagine our staid and stalwart chief of police ever putting a dame behind the wheel of one of his squad cars, but Miss Bliss might not know that. I made sure I was around when Bliss finished her usual Sunday shift and wheeled her way home at around six. I sat in a rickety lawn chair in the front yard of my former motel cottage where I hung my hat and paid my monthly rent.

I kept an eye out for my pet skunk, Ambrosia. She hangs around my place, sometimes sleeping under my cottage, and I put out some burned bacon or other scraps for her. I'd been a little remiss lately, for which I felt guilty. I got up and went into my kitchen and fetched a hard-boiled egg from my fridge. I broke it up in the yard, and pretty soon that damned skunk came around, gave me a dirty look, and downed the egg. She ambled off before Blythe arrived home.

When the lady cop's burgundy Pontiac pulled into the yard next door, I had my sappy smile all ready. She got out of her car and gave me a somewhat suspicious look, but returned my smile readily enough.

"I bought a big bag of sugar when I stopped by the market today," I said, "If you're in need."

"Honey, I've got all the sugar I need. I'm sugar

from head to foot. But I thank you kindly for the offer. What can I be doing for you?"

"Who, me? Nothing in particular. I've just been thinking how I'd like to have a little chat with my neighbor. You know, shoot the breeze. I do hope it's breeze season."

She laughed. "I could use a good jawing. Can I offer you a beer?"

"No, thanks. But by all means go grab one for yourself."

She went into her log cottage and was gone longer than it usually takes to fetch a beer from the refrigerator. When she came back out, she had changed into civvies. Jeans, tennis shoes, and a red checked short-sleeved blouse. She was clutching a Black Label as she collapsed in a lawn chair.

"Anything interesting happen at work today?" I asked, with tremendous innocence.

"Well, I took a big heap of papers out of my In box. And later, I put them in my Out box. Almost took my breath away. What do you think of that?"

"Fascinating. I don't know how you do it. So, everything quiet and peaceful in our fair city, and it's outlying settlements?"

"Couldn't be serener. It's downright homey. Nothing ever happens in Quartz Quarry. Though, if you can believe it, last week the meter maid caught somebody putting slugs in a meter."

"Al Capone used to do that in Chicago. I guess our little burg is so law abiding because of the hawk-like vigilance of our police officers. Of

STEVEN LEROY NELSON

course, there was that little snakebite incident a few days ago."

"I'd completely forgotten about that. Where is my head these days?"

"Atop your lovely shoulders. Tell me if you've heard this one. One of our rural citizens was shot dead through the heart from ambush this morning."

She stopped smiling and gave me a crafty look. "Just an unfortunate accident. Some poor soul's gun went off while he was cleaning it."

"Is that how it was? You know, there's word on the street, and it could be just silliness, that our mayor isn't happy with the number of murders that have occurred in Quartz Quarry in this fine election year. And since he can't figure out a way to get us citizens to get along better, he's simply decided to call murder by a different name. I think he's settled on the word accident."

Blythe's toothy smile was like a fortress. She wasn't going to tell me anything. I needed to play my best card.

"You know, concerning that little accident that took place in Topaz Canyon today. I happen to be the guy who discovered the body."

"Really? That was you? Well, then, that changes things. We can talk about it. It was a homicide, and will be treated like one, mayor or no mayor."

"Are you sure? I've heard the mayor and the chief of police are as inseparable as Siamese twins. And today I witnessed a crime scene investigation

94

of a homicide that looked more like the crime scene investigation of an attempted jay walking."

"Not so. They got what they needed. And they took lots of pictures."

"But they didn't find the murder weapon?"

"Not that I heard. The killer likely took it with him." She took a big swig of beer.

"I guess it'd be a feather in someone's cap to recover that rifle."

"If it was a rifle."

"I heard the shot. It was a rifle. I heard a few of them in the war."

"I'm sorry. I guess we'll recover the murder weapon eventually."

"Yeah. Maybe this week if the right person gets the right information."

"And how would the right person get this information?"

"Maybe just by being a good neighbor. You know, being willing to talk shop a little, in a neighborly way, after work. A little harmless gossip over the fence, although we don't have a fence. Just a bit more news than the average newspaper reader gets."

"I like to talk."

"I know you do. And I mean to chew the fat with you a lot more than in the past."

"That'd suit me fine."

"Good. When's your next day off?"

"Happens to be tomorrow."

"Ever go crystal hunting?"

"As in, crystal ball?"

"No. As in those cute little rock crystals you see around. You see them in shops and such places."

"They're pretty, but I don't go in much for such truck."

"Oh, you should try it. Topaz Canyon is a good spot."

"I don't know if Topaz Canyon is any place for a sweet girl like me. There's a lot going on up there that ought not to be."

"Oh?" I raised my eyebrows. "What, for instance?"

"Hanky panky."

"You don't say? Where are the missionaries when we need them?"

"And poaching, though I guess that's the game warden's lookout."

"Anything else? I'm curious."

"Well," she lowered her voice to a husky whisper, "speaking of crystal balls, I hear there are witches up there. Clovens of them. They dance around in the moonlight, as naked as a new born armadillo."

"I think they're called covens."

"Oh. I thought they were named after you-know-who. Well, they dance around in their bare skin."

"Now you're talking. How would a guy like me get an invite to one of those dances? I cut a rug pretty good."

"I think you'd have to learn how to turn someone into a frog."

"Sister, if I could do that, this town would be full of the little hoppers. But what about you? Do you ever participate in those dances, jigging around it your bare skin?"

"Not this girl. I won't even wear one of those two-piece bathing suits at the water hole."

"You're no fun. I think you've been listening to the wrong people. Topaz Canyon strikes me as a nice, sylvan sort of spot. I think you should head up there tomorrow. Take your gun if you want. I can draw you a map that will take you to an old miner's cabin. Dig around a little. You might find something more interesting than rock crystals."

"Such as?"

"A feather for your cap, maybe."

She gave me a dreamy look. "I could use one of those feathers. A map, you say? Why don't you pick up that feather for yourself? Never hurts for a P.I. to get in good with the police."

"No. I'm too shy and retiring. I don't want all those flashbulbs going off in my face. And the newspaper write-ups would make me turn as red as my car here."

"I've been meaning to ask you about that scarlet locomotive. Where'd you get it?"

"My own car's in the shop, in about a million pieces. This is a loaner from Le Fever's Used Car Gems."

"You couldn't get me to go back to that place. I didn't like the salesman I talked to. Slimy as a hell bender."

"Was he a big loud lad? Travis Spencer?"

"That's him. Gives me the willies, like a bag full of greased snakes."

"I don't care for him either. He probably spends his free time poaching witches for hanky panky."

"Wouldn't surprise me. But you said something about a map."

"Sure." It was getting dark. I fetched a flashlight, a notebook, and a pencil from the glove box of the Nash. Using its hood for a desk, I drew the best map I could and gave it to Blythe.

"Here you go, neighbor. Let me know what you find."

10

The next morning I woke up with something scrabbling around in the back of my mind. It could have been packrats, or it could have been an idea trying to get my attention. I got up and got dressed and tried to think. It didn't work. I applied strong coffee to the problem, but without results. Finally, I lit up a cigar, grabbed my hat, and piled into the Nash. I gave the car its head and it took me in the direction of Vision Quest. Apparently I had a couple of loose ends to tie up. When I walked in, I was greeted by Ann again.

"I just love that yellow shirt."

It's a white shirt. I'm not much for bleach."

"It brings out your amber eyes.'

"I hope it doesn't bring them out too far; I wouldn't want to look like Popeye, him and his damned spinach."

"It'd be a shame to cover up those eyes, but the right pair of sunglasses would emphasize that strong nose."

"What do you have for my strong breath? Odor-killing contacts?"

She laughed — a higher-pitched version of her brother's giggle.

"You're such a funny man, Mr. — ?"

"Hatchett."

"How manly. Can I call you by your first name?"

"Sure. It's Axe. I had pretty violent parents. My sister's name is Scimitar."

"Lovely. So exotic. What can I do for you this fine morning, Axe?"

"Is your brother in? I noticed his Jeep wasn't in the parking lot."

"He probably drove the DeSoto today. He's in the lab, crafting our very high-quality eyeglasses. It's the personal touch that sets us apart from other optical shops, you know."

"Do you keep elves back there?"

The giggle again. "P.D.'s kind of busy this morning, and he gets grumpy when I interrupt him. Can I help you?"

"Maybe so. Say, I just noticed your ring. Is that a pentagram?"

Ann gave me a startled look, and glanced down at her hand. She quickly took the ring off and put it in a pocket of her blazer.

"I didn't mean to wear that to work. Some people are very disapproving."

"Are you a witch? I mean that in the best possible way, of course."

"No. I'm a pagan." A bit of frost had entered her voice. She was almost spitting snowflakes.

"Do pagans belong to covens? You'll have to excuse my ignorance of religion. I used to think Catholics were snake handlers."

"I don't belong to a coven. Now, how can I help you?"

"There are covens up in Topaz Canyon, so I hear. Your sister lives there, but I guess you know that. I've met her."

She defrosted at once. "Wasn't it awful what happened to that poor man? I hope they catch that nasty killer soon. What exactly can I help you with? You mentioned contacts. They make very good ones these days, you know."

"Did you know the murdered man, your sister's neighbor?"

"Slightly. And since you insist on talking about witches, Stu had made some enemies among them."

"Is that so? How did that happen?"

"He broke up one of their moonlight ceremonies. He was out prowling in the woods for some reason. He pointed a gun at them, gathered up their clothes, and sent them home in their cars naked. What a busybody prude! But I guess I shouldn't speak bad about him, since he's dead."

"Sent them home without even their skivvies. I can see how that might upset them. You don't suppose one of those witches shot Slaughter? Out of revenge?"

"There's no chance of that. Witches are gentle, peaceful, people. They're in tune with their earth mother."

"Boy, I wish I was. I always seem to be getting on the wrong side of my earth mother."

"Reading glasses. Do you need reading glasses? We have some that don't make you look like a spinster librarian."

"Careful you don't say things like that around Charlotte."

"She's definitely not a spinster. She's divorced. Twice."

"Before I forget, let me bring up the business that brought me here. A few days ago I brought in a pair of glasses that some poor guy had lost. Did he by any chance show up to get them?"

She gave me a blank look, then a bit of crimson showed on each cheek.

"I don't know anything about that. But that's about par for the course. P.D. frequently keeps me in the dark. Don't ever go to work for your relatives."

"They wouldn't have me."

"I think I'll go fetch my brother for you. I don't care how busy he is. Wait here, please."

She walked stiffly away, keeping her formerly swaying caboose in check.

I looked around. The rock crystals caught my attention again. I remembered the turquoise-colored rock I'd filched from Charlotte's backyard yesterday. For some silly reason I'd kept it in my pocket ever since. Now I looked at the crystals on the shelves to see if there were any like mine. I found a pretty impressive cluster of them, imbedded in a chunk of dirty white quartz. The moment I discovered it, I heard a polite cough behind me. I turned around and found myself confronted with the lab-coat-clad P.D..

"Welcome back," he said, giving me a tight smile. I wondered what Ann had told him about me. "It's Waldenbrook, isn't it?"

"Waldengarver. But let me drop that silliness. I'm a private investigator named Axe Hatchett."

"Why the subterfuge?"

I shrugged. "Sometimes folks don't like talking to detectives. They clam up. I apologize for the game playing. Those specs I brought in the other day, they might belong to someone who tried to drown another someone. A client of mine, now deceased. And the man who might have attacked him is also dead. Murdered. Yesterday."

His eyes opened wide. "My word. My heavens. Are you accustomed to these kinds of happenings in your line of work?"

"More than I'd like to be, believe me. I came in today to see if there was any chance the owner of the orphan glasses ever showed up."

"You could have used the telephone."

"I know, but I'm a face-to-face kind of guy. Besides, I have a rock I wanted to show you. "

His eyes lit up. "Some kind of crystal?"

"Yes." I extracted the rock from my pocket.

There was some pocket lint clinging to it. I blew it off. "What kind of stone is this? And is it worth anything? Is it perhaps rare?"

He took the rock and, to my amazement, licked it. He saw my surprise.

"Sorry. Rock hound's habit. The spittle gives the rock a temporary shine. This is a fine example of an amazonite crystal. It's not worth a great deal, but it's a fine example. Any rock hound would love to have it." He frowned suddenly, then looked puzzled. "Where did you get this?"

"Topaz Canyon. Yesterday."

"That's funny. It's the twin of a piece of amazonite I found a couple weeks ago. It's in my Jeep. I'd go get it right now, but I drove my car to day. I've kept it on the passenger's seat as something to look at while I'm stopped at red lights. Tell me, would you be interested in selling this to me? I'll give you a good price. Though, as I said, it's not all that valuable."

"Actually I'd like to hang on to it."

"Certainly. It's very pretty, and interesting. As to the reason for your being here, no. The owner of the glasses never showed up. However, it's only been a few days."

"But you'll call me if he does show up? You can see how important it might prove to be."

"Yes, of course."

"I notice you're wearing glasses today. Were you wearing contacts the other morning?"

"Yes."

I shook my head. "You couldn't get me to put bits of glass in my eyes."

He gave me his basso profundo giggle. "It's hardly as primitive as that."

"The frames you're wearing look a lot like the ones I brought you."

"Yes. I told you this frame style is very popular."

"They look good. If I wore glasses I might get frames like that myself. Though Ann says gray would look better on me. Because of my war wound. The silver in my hair."

"War wound?"

"You ever eat K Rations?"

"As a matter of fact, yes. I was a corporal in the army."

"I met your other sister a couple of days ago. Nice lady. Have you been up to see her lately?"

"I visit her fairly regularly."

"I have another acquaintance in Topaz Canyon. A friend of both your sisters'. Rolaine LeFever. I believe she told me that you two are acquainted."

"How did my name come up? I've met Mrs. LeFever, through my sisters. I'm terribly sorry about her husband having passed. And what an awful way to die."

"Yes. I guess she was a pretty good friend of this Stu Slaughter guy who owned the snake that killed her husband. And now he's dead. Tragic. Had you heard about it?"

"Certainly. Charlotte lives across the road from

the Slaughter home. She called me. She was pretty broken up. Now, is there anything else I can help you with?"

I could tell I'd worn out my welcome. "Just give me a call if the owner of those glasses shows up." I pulled out my wallet and gave him one of my real business cards. "You can call me at either of those numbers. Thanks for your help."

On my way out, Ann caught my eye. She gave me a stern look, then broke into a girlish smile. "One of these days we're going to sell you something."

I thought maybe her family had already sold me something. A bill of goods.

I stopped by my office for a while. and sat at my desk and willed the phone to ring. It was silent. I cursed it a couple of times. It rang. I should have tried that before.

"Hatchett's Investigations. No nut too hard to crack. Axe speaking."

"It's Bram."

"The check is in the mail. For real."

"I know. I got it. Thanks."

"Look, I don't have any work for you now. I'm barely keeping my head above water."

"I understand. That's not why I'm calling you. I've got something to tell you, and when I've finished telling it, you might not want me working for you again."

That was bad news. I liked Bram. He's invisible. He has the perfect look for an operative. Small, doughy-faced, nondescript. You could look at him for ten minutes, turn your head away for a second, and not remember what he looked like. Perfect, except for his hat. He insists on wearing a big white cowboy hat, about forty gallons worth, with a showy feather in the band. It makes him the most noticeable person for miles. When he's on the job for me, I insist he doesn't wear the hat.

"Spill it," I said.

"Well, it's about that guy that got shot yesterday. Slaughter. I saw it in the paper. I've met that guy. In fact, he threatened me with a gun. I think I might know who killed him."

"That's great news. I'm working on that case myself."

"Then maybe I can help you." He took a deep breath and let it out in a sigh. "It's kind of a long story."

"Give me the Readers' Digest version."

"A little more than a year ago I did something I shouldn't have."

I put my feet up on the desk. "That long? I can scarcely get through a day without doing something I shouldn't."

"I took a job working for poachers."

I took my feet back off the desk, in a hurry.

"What? You poached? You never told me you had a criminal background."

"I really needed the money. You know how it is. I've been sorry for it ever since. I'll never do anything like that again. The worst of it is, we almost got caught. Well, we did, but the guy let us go. It was Slaughter. I had just started working for Happy Trails. You know we have that archery range outside. Well, I was practicing on it one day, on my lunch hour. I'm pretty good with a bow. I'm part Indian, you know."

"I always thought you looked a little like Geronimo. I mean, not so his mother wouldn't know the difference.'

"Celeste says I look like Howdy Doody."

"Yeah, but she's seen you without your makeup. How's the baby coming along?"

"Two more months. Wish I could find some moonlighting to do."

"Maybe you can find a midnight shooting range. Outdoors. Get on with your story."

"OK. There were these two other guys, one of them pretty good, shooting bow and arrow right next to me. We got to talking."

"You weren't wearing ear protection?"

"Huh? Oh, that was a joke."

"If you say so. You got to talking to these guys, then what happened?"

"These guys were bow hunters. Well, it was out of season. They said they wanted to talk to me about something, after work. Said they'd buy me a couple of beers. This one guy said he owned a restaurant, and he had a liquor license. He said to drop by there about seven."

"Where was this place?"

"Jeremiah's Wild Game Grubbery."

"I've heard of it. Nothing good."

"The owner's name is Jerry Clover. The other guy was a car salesman named Travis Spencer."

That pulled me up short for two reasons. Clover was Tracy's last name. And she'd told me her parents owned a restaurant and that she refused to work there. She wouldn't say why. Was Tracy's dad a poacher? Maybe a killer? That might make things inconvenient since I was investigating a murder Old Man Clover might have committed. And as for Travis Spencer...was I never going to hear the last of him? I told Bram none of this.

"This Jerry and Travis fed me more than a couple of beers. More like five, with shots of whiskey to chase down with them. I lost my head. When they got around to telling me their plan, I was too far gone to say no. They did a little poaching on the side, they said. Nothing wrong with it, they said. The woods were full of game, but it was just the government that liked to screw things up for hunters, so they'd made shooting in some seasons illegal. They said they used bows 'cause they didn't make any noise. They had a panel truck to load the carcasses into, and Jerry and Travis said they were planning a trip up Topaz Canyon way. They said there was lots of game up there, and it wasn't much afraid of people. They said they'd pay me something and give me some meat if I agreed to join them.

"Look, I knew it was wrong at the time, but I was a little drunk, and Celeste and I needed money to buy a water heater for the duplex. And I like elk meat."

"So, you were poaching elk."

"Elk, deer, bear, whatever was available. I agreed to go with them. We drove up to Topaz Canyon one bright Sunday, early in the morning. We parked the panel truck off the road, in some trees so nobody would see it, or us. We hiked for a good two or three miles, looking for game. Then we spotted an elk. It was just lying in the shade in a patch of grass. I'm happy to say I'm not the one who shot it. Spencer put an arrow through its lungs before I could even unlimber my bow. The elk crashed through the trees for a short distance and fell over dead. And that's when it happened."

"That's when what happened?"

"That guy Slaughter showed up. We were just starting to gut the elk. He came out of nowhere. None of us heard him coming. He was a tall, wiry, guy, and tough looking. He had a camera on a strap around his neck, and a Colt forty-five revolver on his hip. He came down on us like a ton of buffalo chips."

"Hey, I like that. So, he made you leave the elk? Is that what happened?"

"Yes, and other things. He chewed us out good. Travis went over and took a swing at the guy, but Slaughter put a fist in his face and knocked him on his can. After that, he told us if he ever caught us poaching again, he'd turn us in, or come gunning for us. And then he did the worst thing of all. At gunpoint, he made us carve off big slabs of meat and eat them raw. Jerry and Travis got sick and upchucked the mess."

"And you?"

"I kind of liked it. Must be the Indian blood in me. Celeste thinks our little one might turn out to be a cannibal. Where do women get these ideas?"

"They order them through the mail. What happened next?"

"Nothing. He let us go, without the elk, and with blood all over our faces and shirts. We walked back to the truck. The whole time Travis was cursing the guy, saying how he was going to get even, how he'd make Slaughter eat his own liver. He talked like a savage, a screwy one. Scared me. Jerry, he didn't say so much, but he was pretty hot too."

"How did they think they were going to find Slaughter to wreak their revenge? Did they know who he was? And, if not, how'd you get his name?"

"Jerry knew him. He told us that Slaughter used to hunt rattlesnakes for his restaurant. I remembered the name, that's all"

"I'm glad you're telling me all this, Bram."

"I haven't called the police yet. Should I?"

"No. They're awfully busy people. Let's not be inconsiderate."

"Well, I just had to tell somebody. I sure didn't want the killer getting away with it."

"That won't happen. Thanks for calling me."

"Now that you know about my past, do you think you'll ever let me work for you again?"

"I don't know, Bram. It'll take a while to make up my mind. Don't lose any sleep over it."

"Thanks. Celeste says hello."

No she doesn't, I thought. Bram's wife hated me. She thought I was putting Bram in dangerous situations. Which, as far as I knew, wasn't true.

"There's another thing," said Bram "That Travis, he said he'd beat me into a giant hamburger patty if I ever told anyone about what happened that day."

"Colorful. Do you think he meant it?"

"You should have heard him. You should have seen his face. And he said he'd kill Slaughter if he ever caught him alone and unarmed, which I guess he did. If Travis finds out I talked to you, he — "

"I never reveal my sources, Bram. I've spent more than one lovely night in our local jail for not talking. You're in no danger."

"Good. I mean, I'm glad you don't give up your sources."

We rang off.

11

Coincidence? I hate it. Tracy's Pop. The perennial Travis Spencer. The whole Slabov family. Rolaine. Which of them didn't kill Slaughter? Or was it a group effort? Still, I was glad to get all the information I could. But if Travis had shot Slaughter, why had he waited so long? Maybe he thought the timing was right. Dobie LeFever died at least partly because of Stu. Maybe Travis thought the cops would believe some friend of LeFever's had killed Stu out of revenge. And I doubted if anyone would mistake Travis for a friend of his boss.

In fact, as I thought about it, I wondered if Spencer could have been the one who pushed Dobie into the lake. That would have happened about the same time Spencer had tried to buy the Nash for a cheap price and Dobie had laughed at him. Travis might have considered that the last straw. Or maybe he'd dunked Dobie so he'd be out of the way for Travis to make his big play for Rolaine. Maybe marry her, get control of the business. A beautiful woman and a successful business. Pretty tempting. But I was grooming Slabov for the attempted drowning. The glasses he'd been wearing when I'd seen him today looked exactly like the ones I'd brought to him: same frame, same thick lenses. Wouldn't that be something? P.D. loses his specs while pushing a guy into a lake, and some dumb detective returns them to him.

I decided to check up on Rolaine, see how she was doing. I was sure she knew by now that her old flame had been murdered. Also, this was the day of her husband's funeral; what a swell time she must be having.

I hoped her new lover was consoling her. And I suspected Slabov might be that lover. Rolaine had been kind of cagey when I'd asked her if she knew him. And Slabov had been equally cagey when I'd mentioned LeFever's widow to him. If P.D. was Rolaine's new squeeze, that would give him a motive for getting Dobie out of the way. And according to Rolaine, LeFever didn't believe in divorce But...hell, I was just chasing ideas around in my mind.

I dialed Rolaine's number. It rang a whole lot of times and nobody picked up. Could be the funeral was in progress. Or maybe she just didn't want to talk to anybody right now. My stomach told me I ought to put something in it, and I never argue with it. I realized I had a hankering for wild game, so I grabbed my rat-eared phone book and looked up Jeremiah's Wild Game Grubbery. I got the address and headed for my car.

Jeremiah's is in the middle of Quartz Quarry's small warehouse district. It's housed in an old fake adobe that looks like something big sat on it sometime in the distant past. To my surprise, the adjoining parking lot was almost full. I found a slot to squeeze the Nash into, and went inside. I entered an arched doorway and was hit in the kisser with a smell reminiscent of old campfires and even older grease. There was a loud clashing of cutlery and of gnashing teeth.

Outside of the main dining room was a long lunch counter that looked like a good spot for me. I found an empty stool. Next to me was a stringy, hard-bitten woman gnawing on somebody's ribs. On her hard bicep was the tattooed legend, "Property of Lizard." On the other side of her was a portly, gray-bearded fellow with a beer gut and a blue-veined, bulbous nose. Perhaps the great Lizard himself.

The light was dim, but the décor wasn't worth seeing anyway. There were a bunch of mangy animal hides tacked to the walls, interspersed with some canvases smeared with oils presumably meant to depict various western landscapes. There were a couple of old flintlock rifles residing on the wall above the billboard-sized menu behind the lunch counter.

I had only just finished enjoying all this when a plump middle-aged woman in a deerskin apron bustled out from the kitchen to ask if I was ready to order, or still needed a few minutes. Except for her sunny smile, she was the perfect image of Tracy. At least, Tracy in twenty years or so. Mom's name tag proclaimed her to be Lilly. I was so tongue-tied in the presence of my amata's mama that I could barely stammer out an order for the armadillo burger with the trout caviar relish and prickly pear fries. While my food was preparing I listened to the wholesome music of hungry diners champing the bones of exotic prey. It made me hungrier than I'd already been.

A couple dressed roughly like Wild Bill Hickock and Calamity Jane entered the Grubbery. They passed through a broad arch that led to the main dining room. They needed a broad arch, and would likely need a broader one when they came back out. Jeremiah's was obviously one of those all-you-can-eat, stack-it-high-on-the-platter, kind of places. When Mom Clover brought out my food, I thought they must have used the entire armadillo, and maybe a cousin, too.

"How's that looking to you?"

"Like Thanksgiving. Tell me, Lilly, is Mr. Clover around?"

"Dumpling, he had to go pick up a buffalo. Why those folks can't deliver I'll never know. He should be in shortly. Maybe before you've tucked away your dessert." She leaned heavily on the counter, showing a furrow of cleavage as long as my neck tie. "We got homemade mince pie today. Made with genuine antelope suet." She winked.

"Oh, boy. I'll try to save room."

She went down the row of lunch counter customers, taking dessert orders, filling coffee cups — I was happy to see she shared her daughter's generous habit of over-filling the cups — and chatting in a folksy, friendly fashion. I'd noticed a silver charm bracelet on her pudgy, freckled, arm. Among the usual miniature poodles, tennis rackets, hearts and Liberty Bells, I'd seen a black and silver pentagram. Was Tracy's mom a witch? Jeez! A witch for a mom, and a poacher and possible murderer for a dad. It explained a lot. Any vague notions I'd had about marriage flew out of my head like a flock of frightened buzzards.

I was still trying to wrap my taste buds around my lard-laden lunch, when a stubby man with a frizzy gray beard, a fringed leather jacket, and a coonskin cap strode in from the kitchen. He must have come in through a back door. He had some of Tracy's facial features, but none of the good ones. He tied on a cowhide apron with the spotted hair still on, then walked right up to me.

"The Misses tells me you're looking for me."

"Mr. Clover?"

"Call me Jerry."

I shook his hand. To my surprise, there was no fur on the palm.

"My name's Astro Craven, but my friends call me Snake Bane."

"Well, Snake Bane, I'm your friend, ain't I?"

"I reckon so."

"How can I help you?"

"I got a business proposition. I heard on the snake vine you might be looking for a new provider for rattlers, maybe a Gila monster or two. Heard your last provider had an accident."

He frowned, apparently in deep thought. "No, sir. My snake man's still hale and hearty."

"You sure? Didn't Stu Slaughter used to bring you rattlers?"

"Son, that was years ago. I fired Slaughter when I caught him trying to rustle one of my yearling steers out to the Three Clovers Ranch. I can't abide a thief. I unlimbered my hoss pistol right then and there, and shot the heels off that no good's boots. I read in the paper the fellow died, and I don't mean to speak ill of those that's gone to their reward, but I had no use for the varmint."

"Well, looks like the snake vine failed me this time. Looks like I might have to invest in one of those telephone gadgets. Sorry to take up your time."

"Not at all. It's been a pleasure. First visit to our little grubbery?"

"Sure is, Jerry. But it won't be my last."

"Glad to hear it. Glad to hear it. Can I fill up your coffee mug? Have you saved room for dessert?"

"I surely can't eat another bite. But I'll take you up on that mince pie next time I'm in."

"Happy to hear it, Snake Bane." He reached across the counter and slapped me on the back like he thought I was choking on my armadillo. Then he excused himself and headed into the dining room to glad hand more customers. Lilly came and rang me up, pouting at my refusal of pie.

I went back to the office. I tried calling Rolaine again. Someone answered, but it wasn't her.

"Is this Charlotte?" I asked.

"Yes. Is this Mr. Mitten, or, whatever your name is?"

"Axe Hatchett. I'm a private detective. Sorry for the subterfuge. Sometimes it's necessary in my business."

"You're forgiven. Let me get Rolaine."

I waited a minute.

"Axe? Life is a nightmare." Those were her first words to me. "Is it my fault? That both Dobie and Stu are dead?"

"Of course not. You're in no way to blame for either death. It's just unfortunate you knew both victims."

"Thank you. I made it to the funeral. I couldn't have done it without Charlotte and Ann. They both took off work early to be with me. We just got back from running some errands and walking in the park. What are you doing for dinner?"

The question took me off guard. My armadillo burger was sitting in my stomach like a stone Buddha.

"I don't have any plans. I just finished lunch."

"Why not come up here and have dinner with me and Charlotte and Ann? Or are you afraid to be the only boy?"

"Scared to death. I'll wear my bullet proof vest. Dinner at your place sounds fine. But are you sure you really want me? Wouldn't I be interrupting?"

"No. I want you here. I want to talk to you, about — things. I just brought home a bunch of groceries. I'll fix you a nice dinner. The ladies can help. Say, six o'clock?"

"That works for me. Can I bring anything?"

"Just yourself. Come up earlier if you like. We can talk while dinner's cooking."

"OK. I'll be happy to come. I'll see you at a little before six."

"Drive carefully."

I said goodbye, hung up, and thought about things. No doubt, Rolaine would want to talk about Slaughter's murder. Right now I didn't know what I'd tell her. I had scarcely a clue about who might have killed Stu. I could think of some possible suspects, including Rolaine and Ann. Charlotte was in the clear, but her brother P.D. wasn't. At least we'd all be in favor of accusing Travis Spencer. But it could make for a pretty nervous evening.

I was also concerned about Tracy. She'd likely want me to drop by Rocko's for my supper. How was I going to break the news to her that I'd be standing her up to dine with three attractive females? I began to dread the evening. And what was I supposed to do until six o'clock? I decided to drop by and see Tracy before I went up to Topaz Canyon. It was the least I could do.

I went home and showered and changed clothes first. I put on something a little less shabby and wrinkled than what I'd been wearing, but I didn't put on my nicest clothes. I didn't want Tracy to get any wrong ideas about my intentions concerning the widow and her friends.

As I drove over to Rocko's, I wondered if I should tell her I was seriously thinking of trading for the Ruby Roadrunner. That might help the bitter pill of my dinner date go down a little sweeter. Or, should I save it for a surprise? I couldn't decide.

By the time I pulled up in front of the diner — how few customers did this place have, anyway? — I was already thinking about the Slaughter murder again. And the LeFever "accident". I hoped I'd get home from Rolaine's early enough to have a chat with Blythe Bliss. I knew she was one of those saps who gets up at dawn and goes to sleep at nine. Maybe I'd go ahead and wake her up. But that was stupid. I could always talk to her in the morning. I walked into Rocko's.

12

"Hello, my little Potato Flower," she greeted me. "What'll it be today? Egg sandwiches, or a burger? I'll get the fresh coffee going."

She was smiling big. I felt like a heel. OK, I was a heel.

"Nothing, Tracy. Just coffee, my little Miss Fortune Cookie. I need to talk to you about a little something."

"Why no chow? You on a diet?"

"You saying I need one?"

"Only here and there. You're fine. But you're usually hungry."

"I had lunch at Jeremiah's Wild Game Grubbery."

"Oh. Now I understand. You really ate at my Mom and Pop's place? Did you meet my folks?"

"Both of them."

"Well? What'd you think? Did you tell them we're engaged?"

"We're not engaged."

"Did you tell them we're going to be?"

"I didn't tell them anything. I was working. I was incognito."

"You like that stuff. I thought you were working on a murder case."

"I am. Possibly a double murder."

"So, you're trying to tell me my folks are murderers?" She started wiping down the counter with her favorite rag. The one she inherited from Paul Revere's bartender.

"No, not exactly. Your dad might be involved with a poacher who might be involved with a killing."

"Sure. Poaching, lying, shop-lifting, tax evasion. That's my Pop for you. He's been all those things. But not a murderer, Axe. He doesn't kill folks."

"I didn't say he did. Say, is it true your mom's a witch?"

"You're batting a thousand, Bub. My Mom's a Methodist. What are you talking about?"

"Just that I noticed she was wearing a charm bracelet. One of the charms was a pentagram."

"Land O Goshen! I guess I was lucky she didn't sacrifice me when I was a baby. Listen, what other kinds of charms were on that bracelet? Let me sit down so I don't faint."

"Cookie will fire you if you sit down. The charm bracelet had the usual sappy stuff on it. Baby booties, a tennis racket, a kite with a little silver chain for a tail."

"Oh. So Mom's expecting, she plays tennis, and

she's Ben Franklin. Quit playing detective. Mom might not even know what a pentagram is. Maybe she bought it because it was cute. Maybe somebody gave it to her."

"OK. Don't climb all over me."

"Never in public, my little Wormy Apple. Say, why are you dressed so nice? It's not my day off. We don't have a date."

I cleared my throat. There was a great big frog in it.

"I got to go to a meeting later."

"One of those Private Eyes Anonymous things, probably."

"I'll be eating dinner. With a client. And a couple of other people."

She gave me a menacing glare. Tracy's very good at those.

"A dinner. With a client. And you're wearing your Little Lord Fauntleroy outfit. Is this client the Widow LeFever?"

"Of course. You know that's who I'm working for."

"You've seen her?"

"Only once."

"Hair like Rapunzel's? Eyes like twin moons reflecting off a lake?"

"Naw, nothing like that. She's small and dark. Just a garden variety widow, that's all."

"Not even a little pretty?"

"I wouldn't say that. She's OK, if you like the type."

"And of course you don't. Who are the two other diners? Tell me they're men."

"Not entirely."

"One man, one woman. A nice happy married couple."

"Two women, both single as far as I know. But one of them's a librarian."

"So? I've seen librarians that make Rita Hayworth look like a male gym teacher."

"The other one's a witch."

"Like Mom. Check out her bracelet for me. I'll bet it's charming."

"Come on, Tracy, this is important. Two of the women are suspects. And two of them are the sisters of a suspect. I could learn a lot. And I didn't exactly wrangle myself an invitation. Rolaine — Mrs. LeFever — asked me to come to dinner. Her husband's funeral was today. I came in here to tell you about it so you don't get the wrong idea."

She softened a little, and when she poured my coffee she didn't put it my lap.

"Just watch yourself, Buster. You know, we have some pretty good-looking guys come into Rocko's. One came in this morning who was the spitting image of Robert Mitchum."

"Probably looking for his next leading lady. Did you tell him you could act?"

"No, because that would be like cheating on my boyfriend. I'm not that kind of floosy."

"Look, I'll keep my eyes on my plate the whole time. And I'll leave as soon as it's polite."

"You better. In fact, you can even be a little rude. I'm not asking you to do something that doesn't come natural."

I escaped Tracy with my head intact, and started my trip up through Topaz Canyon to Rolaine's place. I thought of stopping off and picking up a nice bottle of wine, or some flowers. A guy with class would do that. But then, we're talking about me.

There hadn't been any more rain, and the dirt road was dry and easy to navigate. There were two cars parked in the wide space of gravel next to Rolaine's house: Ann's green pickup truck, looking dusty, and Charlotte's yellow Jeepster, looking freshly washed. I parked my boat in the only space left over, and had to make two tries to fit it in. I climbed the steps to the front door, and it opened before I could even knock.

Charlotte let me in. She was friendly and held a drink in one hand. It looked like a big martini. Some kind of jazz music was coming from the hi fi, a little louder than necessary. Charlotte was wearing a long black dress, black open-toed shoes, and jet jewelry.

"Come in, Mr. Hatchet. Or, is it Mitten? Or Waldenburg?"

"Waldengarver. Don't get my aliases mixed up; I work hard on them. You ladies been talking about me?"

"Yes. And about a hundred other things. Come in. Can I take your jacket?"

"I'll leave it on, thanks. It hides the ketchup stains on my shirt."

Ann came in from the kitchen. Her face was a bit flushed, and she, too, held a drink. An amber number with ice. She wore black pants, a white frou-frouey blouse, and a short black jacket. She came up very close and friendly, and planted a wet kiss on my cheek that I decided Tracy would never hear about .

"Our hero detective! Find a chair and I'll find you a drink. What'll be?"

"Coffee, if you got it."

"Coffee? What kind of a tough-guy drink is that? I make a mean Manhattan."

"No. It might be too mean. I'm kind of a soft guy. Coffee will do."

"I'll get some going." She disappeared into the kitchen, swaying her hips nicely for me. Maybe it was my aftershave. I decided I'd have to buy another jug of Drunken Sailor's Rum Musk.

Rolaine peeked into the living room as I selected a severe looking armchair near the fireplace where an infant fire was burning. She held a gleaming chrome percolator in one slim hand, and a drink, something clear and tall, in the other. She wore a frilly white apron over a black suit that hugged her figure nicely. Everybody was wearing black. Oh, yeah, the funeral.

"Welcome back to my humble abode. I'm glad you're early; dinner's almost ready. How was your drive up?"

"Curvy. But I don't mind curves."

"I'll bet you don't." She actually winked at me. How much had these girls been drinking?

Rolaine went back into the kitchen and Charlotte took her place. She sat down in the chair opposite mine and looked dreamily at the fire.

"Do you ever read children's books?" she asked me.

"No. But I'm getting pretty good with my alphabet, and I can write my name with hardly any mistakes."

She giggled. The Slabov family sure liked their giggles. She rose from her chair and fetched a big kid's book from the hassock near the coffee table and handed it to me. It looked horrifying. The cover illustration showed a scared-to-death looking little boy in pajamas, sitting up in bed. He was staring at a monster that looked like it was made from somebody's dirty laundry. The book was called, Rumpled Sheetskin Drops By To Say Howdy. The author was some chucklehead calling himself Xavier Zoo.

"Is that the guy's real name?" I asked.

"It is. Can you believe it? He's my favorite children's author. This is his newest. I brought it up to show Ann, see if her girls might like to read it."

"I shouldn't think any kid would want to read such a book. Is the writer related to Mary Shelly?"

Another giggle. "The children love him. They can't get enough of the lovable Zoo. He frightens the freckles right off them. Believe me, there are kids with five-hundred watt nightlights in their rooms because of Zoo. He's like a cross between Dr. Seuss and Mr. Hyde. I suspect he'll end up in an insane asylum eventually, surrounded by his creations: Closet Creep; Mothball Man; Under-the-Bedlam-Beast."

"Sounds like a swell guy to sic on your offspring."

"Parents don't like him, but you've got to let children pick out their own books. Otherwise, they won't read. I don't have offspring myself. Two failed marriages and no kids. At least I get to be Aunty to Ann's little girls. They're cute and sweet. Not at all like their dad. Ann's still legally married, but Brad's out of the picture. What about you? Married? Ten kids?"

"Single. No kids."

"Girlfriends?"

"One. I think it's kind of serious, but don't tell her I said so."

Ann joined us. She sat down on the hassock. "Dinner's about on the table. I hope everyone's hungry."

"I am," I said, "even though I had an armadillo for lunch. What are we having? It smells good."

She counted off on her fingers. Her nails were painted bright pink. "Salad. Salisbury steak. Peas and carrots. Jell-O with grated vegetables. Rolls. Chocolate cake for dessert."

"Sounds swell. No wonder it smells good."

She leaned toward me, her eyes too bright. "Do

I smell good, too?"

I caught a whiff of perfume. It wasn't bad, but it couldn't compete with the Salisbury steak. I drew back a couple of inches. I caught Charlotte rolling her eyes.

"Ann has a new boyfriend," she explained. "It makes her very — romantic."

"What makes you think I have a new beau?" asked Ann.

"Because you're so happy. And you're more careful about your hair and your makeup when you've got a man in your life."

"It's none of your business, really."

"No. I'm only your sister. Your older sister."

"Like you ever let me forget it."

Rolaine interrupted us to announce dinner. We filed through a short hallway and into a dining room with lots of windows overlooking the back-yard and garden where Rolaine and I had taken our stroll. There was a white-blond table and chairs, and a matching buffet and china cupboard. The dishes were white china with some simple pattern in rose. I was made to take the chair at the head of the table. Dobie's chair, I thought, and it made me squirm a little.

The food was good, although I could have done without the Jell-O embedded with cabbage, car-rots, onions, and God knows what else. The con-versation quickly zeroed in on Dobie and Stu. That was fine with me; I hoped to pick up some new information. I was surprised when Charlotte openly admitted to having been Stu's lover.

"It was mostly physical," she said, when the subject came up. "A good arrangement for both of us. Stu didn't like getting close to other people, and I'm not looking for anyone to get too serious about. I'm not like Ann. She's a pillow-talk kind of girl. She's a 'tell me your biggest secret and I'll tell you mine' type. That's why she gets her heart broken."

"I'm not as cold as you are, Charlotte. We can't all turn off our emotions like you can. And I'll thank you not to discuss my love life with just anyone." She sounded mad and hurt. Charlotte was sitting to my left, Ann to my right. Strangely, I thought, Rolaine was at the foot of the table.

Charlotte arched her eyebrows at me.

"Do you hear, Axe? We're not to discuss delicate matters in front of you. How does that make you feel? A welcome guest? My view is, you're a detective, and you've been hired to investigate Stu's murder. So just how long would it take you to discover that every woman at this table has been Stu Slaughter's lover at one time or another?"

"Not long. But I'd keep such information to myself as much as possible."

Charlotte looked at Ann. "See, you have nothing to worry about. Mr. Hatchett will keep your little secret. It's OK if he knows I was sleeping with Stu right up until the time of his death. It's OK if he knows you were the lover that came before."

"Because you stole him from me."

"Not that again. Please. I did not steal him from you. It was his idea. And thanks to your secrecy in such matters, I didn't even suspect you and Stu had slept together. Don't make me out to be worse than I am."

All three ladies had refreshed their drinks since my arrival. Their faces were flushed, and there was a lot of emotion showing right below the surface. I was glad I'd brought my revolver.

"You're worse than me," Ann accused. "I don't steal boyfriends, and I keep my private life private. I have my little girls to think about."

"I have my job to think about. But I see no reason why we can't mention our love lives in front of Axe. Hasn't it occurred to you, Ann, that you might be a suspect in Stu's murder?"

"You're horrible. Why are you doing this?"

"I guess that makes me a suspect, too," said Rolaine, very quietly. "Although, if I was guilty, why would I hire a detective to track down Stu's killer?"

"Maybe you're just being clever," said Charlotte. "I think you could have done it. Gone outside, I mean. Slithered under my porch with a rifle. You've told me yourself that Dobie taught you how to shoot. Or was it Stu? Anyway, your agoraphobia is much less debilitating than it was."

"Thanks to you," said Rolaine. "So, I guess you've helped make me a murder suspect."

"I think you killed Stu, Charlotte" said Ann.

"I couldn't have. I have an alibi. I was at work when Stu was shot. Ask Axe. He called me at work to come rescue Ernie."

"I was home by myself," said Rolaine. "I have no alibi."

"And you, Ann? Where were you?" asked Charlotte.

"How dare you! I was — I was at church. I dropped the girls off at Mom's that morning, and I went to church."

"Which church? I know you like to play the field, looking for the right spiritual haven. And I know you don't always go to church on Sundays. That's just what you tell Mom so she'll take care of Angel and Brie. I'll bet you were with your new lover that day. Unless you were killing your old one."

"Ladies, please." Rolaine's voice was calm, but with a ragged edge. "Let's not argue. Obviously, none of us shot poor Stu. Let's have a nice dinner and relax. Axe, I apologize."

"Don't apologize on my account. You ladies have had a rough time of it lately. I understand. But it's true that I didn't come here to watch a box-ing match."

"Ann's strictly a light weight," said Charlotte.

"I'd rather be that than a heavy weight like you."

"Girls! Please." Rolaine stood up. "Let's have our cake and coffee in the living room. Shall we?" We all helped her to clear the table and carry things into the kitchen. We became a bit more civilized over our chocolate cake. Dessert sometimes brings out the best in people. But Charlotte wasn't quite finished needling Ann.

"Heard from Brad lately?" she asked her.

"Of course, Charlotte. He's still my husband, and my children's father. He watched Angel and Brie on Saturday. They had a nice time."

"Where were you? Mom's?"

"I went out. I wanted to be alone. Is that all right with you?"

"Of course. Do you think you and Brad will ever get back together?"

"No. It's too late." Ann's already flushed face darkened, and her lavender eyes flashed angrily. "I don't know what P.D. told Brad about me — a bunch of lies — but he'll never look at me the same way again."

"Ann, that's all in your head. You're just jealous that P.D. goes hunting with Brad and not you."

"That's stupid. Why would I be? I've gone hunting with our brother tons of times."

"But not recently. P.D. has his own life now. It's not how it was when we were kids. I don't believe P.D. said anything about you to Brad. That was just Brad's excuse for leaving you. I think he was seeing somebody else. Really, it's hard to believe he had anything to do with creating your two wonderful little girls."

"Are you suggesting he's not their father?"

"Of course not. I'm only saying — "

"Time to change the subject," said Rolaine "Actually, I've got some questions I'd like to ask Axe about the investigation." She turned to me. "Any new developments?"

"Well, it depends. As far as your husband's death is concerned, I'm sorry to say I doubt we'll ever know if it was truly an accident. I wish I could tell you differently, but that's the way it looks. As for Stu's murder, I've added a couple of suspects to the investigation. I've got a lead or two I'm working on. I hope to hear some news from a contact of mine tonight. In fact, I should really be getting on my way home. It's not that I'm not enjoying myself, but — "

"I'm sorry," Charlotte broke in. "It's my fault. Mostly mine. I've been a bitch this evening. Maybe Stu's death meant more to me than I realized."

"It's my fault too," said Ann. "I probably shouldn't have had so many drinks. I let my sister get under my skin. Just like when we were kids. Sorry."

"Not at all. It's been a nice evening, and the meal was swell. I really mean it when I say there's someone I need to talk to tonight." I stood up and faced my hostess. "Thanks for everything. I'll be in touch. I hope to crack this case, and it won't be too long before I manage it."

All three women walked me to the door.

"Thanks for coming," Rolaine said, offering me her hand.

"It was nice getting to know you better," said

Ann, offering me her hot cheek. I barely brushed it with my mustache.

"I'll walk you to your car," said Charlotte. "I wouldn't want you getting pushed into a lake, or shot, or anything."

13

We walked down the front steps side by side. When I got to my car and had the driver's door open, she said, "I wasn't very nice in there, was I? Do you have brothers or sisters?"

"No. I'm an only child. I think my folks were pretty relieved."

"Sometimes it's difficult to be an adult around Ann. It's like we're kids again. She's my bratty little sister, and I'm her condescending big sister. I guess it'll never change. I'm nicer to P.D. I don't know how he can have Ann working for him. I'll bet she's a brat around him, too. Goodnight. Good luck with your investigation."

"Thanks. And goodnight to you."

"One more thing, if you don't mind. Do you think Dobie's death had anything to do with Stu's?"

"I think there's a chance, but I really don't know. It's possible some friend of Dobie's killed Stu out of revenge. It's also possible the killer wants us to believe just that. Maybe the two deaths are completely unrelated. Now, let me ask you one, about your sister. She's a pagan. Does she ever dance around with the witches?"

Charlotte giggled. "Haven't I given away enough of my sister's secret's? It's kind of funny, really. If I'd found out about it sooner, I don't think I would have had anything to do with Stu. He was kind of a vigilante, I guess.

"Anyway, Ann finally told me not only that she'd been Stu's lover, but how they met. Ann isn't really a witch, or even a pagan. Not in a serious way. But she did go dancing in the moonlight once, with a coven of witches, right here in Topaz Canyon.

"They danced nude. Stu came along with a gun and gathered up their clothes, and sent everybody home that way. Except he didn't send Ann home. He took her, naked, to his place. Ann thought it was kind of romantic."

"I'm guessing some of those witches were pretty steamed. Did any of them try to get their revenge on Stu that you ever heard of?"

She shook her head. "They're a pretty namby-pamby bunch from what I've heard. Even the men."

"There are men witches?"

"Sure. And some of them aren't even fruits. Are you thinking one of them could have shot Stu? I doubt it. Besides, Ann said that little dance was months and months ago. If some witch was going to get even with Stu, why wait so long?"

"Getting back to what I already said, the killer might have wanted Stu's murder to look like revenge for Dobie LeFever's accidental death."

"I'm glad I don't have to solve the case. I'll stick with being a librarian. Good night again."

"Sure. Good night. Don't read any of those Xavier Zoo books before you go to bed."

I drove too fast on the way home, wanting to get there before Blythe Bliss laid her curly head on her pillow, but I had nothing to worry about. She was waiting for me. I'd forgotten to switch on my porch light, but hers was glowing a warm yellow.

She was sitting in her lawn chair, a Black Label in one hand, two dead soldiers at her fair feet. She was wearing a pastel print sack dress and sandals. Her hair was loose on her shoulders.

I looked at the dead soldiers as I got out of the car, then her feet. She crossed her legs. I looked at those, then at her face. She wore the smile of a woman who knows she has a few charms to play with.

"Where you been this late?" she asked, in her nasal twang.

"A man's got to work, you know."

She sniffed the air. "I smell three kinds of perfume. And I think, gin. Do I have to call the vice squad on you?"

"Nonsense. You're only smelling my feet. They're like flowers." I dragged my own tired lawn chair a little closer to Blythe. "How was your day off? Did you find any crystals?"

"No. But your map was good. I found an old military rifle, a thirty-caliber M1 carbine, with a folding stock. It'd been fired recently. I turned it in. It'd been wiped clean of fingerprints, but there were some partials on the cartridges remaining in the clip.

"They shot the rifle into a barrel of water or something. They think the slug matches the one that killed Slaughter. But they're sending it off somewhere, maybe Washington, to make sure."

"Did you get the feather in your cap you were hoping for?"

"I did, though it could have worked out better. I'm not complaining, though, and I thank you kindly."

"How could it have gone better?"

"Right before I left the department — I was sticking around to see what would happen — the guy who owns the gun called us."

"Did he confess?"

"No, honey, he didn't. He called to report the gun stolen. He said he noticed it was missing from his Jeep when he went to look for some rock that he thought he'd left on the seat. Funny name. Let's see if I can remember. Philo Dexter Slabov. Sounds like a Gypsy to me."

You could have knocked me over with a lead feather. "I've met the guy."

"Of course you have. You've got all kinds of connections. You know, I like sitting here talking to you. This could be the start of a beautiful friendship, as they say in that Western."

"Don't get any ideas. I'm spoken for, and the speaker is a screecher."

"I'm not trying to do any poaching. I'm like you. I think we can help each other. I think you and me should be more neighborly, like you said."

"You got anything more to tell me, neighbor?"

"They took that fellow's prints, the Gypsy's, and they matched the partials on the cartridges. But I guess that makes sense. He's pretty clever, but I'm surprised he doesn't have an alibi. He says Sunday was his day off, and his shop is closed, but he went in to work anyway, to get caught up on something, and he was by himself the whole time."

"You think he did it? Why would he report the rifle stolen? There's no way you would have traced it to him. There's a million of those old Army Surplus rifles. It doesn't make sense. You think he was being clever, huh?"

"Yes. It makes him look innocent."

"Maybe. Did you lock the guy up?"

"Of course not. We can't prove he did anything. Not yet. But we're going to keep an eye on him, and he better not try to leave town. Don't you worry — the Quartz Quarry Police Department always gets its man."

"What if the killer turns out to be a woman?"

"Then the Quartz Quarry Police will get her. You can bet on it."

"That brings up a question I've got for you. Those witches you talked about yesterday. Do any of them ever act up, give you any trouble?"

"They're a pretty harmless bunch. Peaceful little heathens."

"I think they call themselves pagans."

"Six of one, half-a-dozen of the other."

"Did you know there's such things as men witches?"

"They don't wear the black dresses or the pointy hats."

"No, on the level. Men witches."

"I know. I've seen a couple. There's even one that's kind of a thorn in our sides, now that you mention it. Gets drunk a lot. He's a brawler, too. We ran him in for a hit and run once."

"Sounds like a tough customer. I don't suppose you know his name?"

"I do."

"But you're not telling. I'm your neighbor, remember. Don't forget about the map I drew for you."

"Why would you want to know some witch's name? It's Sponk. Eldon Sponk."

"Know where I could find him?"

"Try the phone book. I don't know where he lives."

"He's a brawler and a boozer. Can you think of any bars where he might be a regular?"

"Soupy's Rot Gut Bucket. You know the place?"

"Who doesn't? It's notorious. They won't let

you in if you're not wearing brass knuckles. I'm not sure if I want to go into that place by myself or not. Care to come with me? In street clothes?"

"Not even for you, honey."

"Well, I don't blame you. Listen, thanks for the information, sister. It's past your bedtime, isn't it? I see you're doing a little celebrating."

"It's 'feather in my cap' day. You be careful at Soupy's, you hear? When were you thinking of going?"

"Tomorrow."

"Go early, when there aren't so many brawlers. I don't want to be scraping you off their floor with a putty knife and a scrub brush."

"I'll dress up as a nun. That ought to keep me safe."

"Not in Soupy's. Some masher will want to dance with you. Goodnight, y'all. It's Blythe's bed time."

I told her goodnight and went into my own cottage, first bringing in my mail from the mailbox. When I got inside I looked at the stuff. Bills, ads, and a little box wrapped in brown paper and with no return address.

I took out my jack knife and cut through the packing tape. Inside the box was something wrapped in tissue paper. I unwrapped it. I found myself staring at something that stared right back.

It was a glass eye, with a gray-blue iris. As I held it up to the light, it seemed to glimmer and glint. Almost wink.

Stu Slaughter's eye. It had to be. But who had sent it to me? The killer...who else? But was it a warning, or a taunt?

I put the thing back in the box and went to bed.

14

I didn't sleep all that well that night. When I got up the next morning, I didn't shave. I hoped it made me look tougher.

I left my five-shot Chief's thirty-eight on the night stand and strapped on my thirteen-shot Browning High Power in a shoulder holster and hid it under a ratty sports coat I got from the back of the closet. I added scuffed-up shoes with my baggy pants. Then I looked in the mirror.

I looked like a bum, but kind of a tough one. Then, for no reason I could think of, I dug the glass eye out of its box and slipped it into my jacket pocket. Maybe it would bring me good luck.

At around ten o'clock, I headed out for Soupy's. It was one of those dives that opens early to catch the hard-core rummy crowd: the folks who can't tie their shoes until they've had a snort or two. I didn't like the idea of parking the fancy Nash in Soupy's unsavory neighborhood, so I parked it in a lot about ten blocks away and walked the rest of the distance. Soupy's front door was wide open; flies were welcome too.

I was lucky. There were only three customers in the place this early: two old ladies dressed in their grandmothers' clothes and lapping at tall beers, and a haunted-looking young guy so skinny you could have used him for a television antenna. His hands were wrapped around a tumbler with about two inches of hooch the color of motor oil. Every once in a while I saw him lift the glass to his chattering teeth and empty it. The barkeep kept pouring another three fingers of whiskey into the guy's tumbler, which sloshed around a lot when he picked up the glass. Poor bastard.

The bartender himself was pretty scary. He was about the size of a prize bull, with a bristly red crew cut, angry pop eyes, and biceps as big around as car tires. I took a stool and he came over to see what I wanted. He carried a bar rag that would have made Tracy weep with joy.

"What'll be, Mack?" His voice was as raspy as the back of a porcupine.

"Coffee."

He made a face. It was even worse than his regular one. "It's too early for coffee. How about a beer?"

"OK, I'll buy a beer. You can drink it while I have my coffee."

"I'd have to make the coffee."

"So make it. You look strong enough. I'll buy you two beers."

He shrugged, then turned around and fussed and grumbled over an ancient coffee urn, adding water and coffee grounds. When he turned back around, he selected a couple of marginally clean beer schooners, filled them with beer from the tap, and cut the foam off them with a forefinger that looked and smelled like a big pickle. As I watched, he drank them down one at a time then licked his bovine lips.

"Thanks," he said. "Coffee's done." He found a crockery mug and filled it with what I honestly believe he thought was coffee and pushed it over to my side of the bar. "Sugar? I don't have no cream."

"Black's fine." I sampled the brew. It was hot and dark brown. "Thanks." I drank it in silence, which was hard because it made me want to scream.

The skinny guy had emptied his tumbler again, so the barkeep moved over to him and poured out another couple of inches of saddle varnish. When he came back my way I started talking.

"I'm looking for a guy named Eldon Sponk."

"So?"

"I couldn't find him in the phone book, but I heard he comes in here often. Seen him lately?"

"This Eldon Sponk guy?"

"Yeah. That's the one."

His face was a model of battered stoicism. "Lots of guys come in here. Soupy's is a jumping place. I can't say as I'd recognize your friend if I saw him."

Here's a little etiquette problem that's always bothered me. How much should you give as a bribe? Does it depend on the value of what you're buying, or the class of the joint you're in at the time? I slipped a silver dollar across the scratched bar top. Everything in the place was scratched. The round tables, the mismatched chairs, the beat-up oak floor, even the pictures on the girlie calendar that hung behind the bar. A whole lot of scratching must go on in Soupy's.

"That for the coffee and beer?"

"Yeah." I pushed another dollar in his direction.

"Is that it?" he asked, almost sneering at the money.

"How much do you think it's worth, pal? I'm only asking you to tell me when a regular customer is coming in next." I grabbed back one of the dollars and started to put it away.

"Wait." He held up a big hand, palm forward, like a cop directing traffic. "Tonight. He'll be in tonight."

I gave him back the dollar. "You sure?"

"Yeah. He works here."

I thought of something. "What about a guy named Stu Slaughter? He ever come in here?"

He shook his head. "Folk's don't mention their name's a lot in here. What's he look like?"

"About forty. Short gray hair. Tall and thin, but muscular. Face like a handsome sledge hammer."

"Ain't ringing no bells."

I started to get off my stool. My hand brushed against my outside coat pocket and I felt the bulge of the glass eye.

"This Slaughter guy, he used to wear this in his face." I flashed the eye at him, holding it iris up on my palm. To my amazement, the bartender started to laugh.

"Now I know the guy. Best fight I ever saw. Right here in Soupy's. Eldon and this guy. Bare knuckles. They bashed at each other for half-an-hour. I thought they was both going to end up in the morgue. Eldon slugged this bruiser so hard his damned glass eye popped out and bounced across the floor. Guy didn't even pay attention. Kept pounding on Eldon. Wiped up the floor with him. Sent him to the croaker's. This guy did that to Eldon. Can you believe it?"

"I'm looking forward to meeting this Eldon of yours. You at all curious how I got Stu Slaughter's eye?"

"None of my damned business. You want more coffee? I could use another beer."

I took my piddling amount of information and left the place. I walked the ten blocks back to my car and headed over to Rocko's. On the way I tried on P.D. Slabov as Slaughter's killer. His rifle, his bullet, his fingerprints. Maybe a motive. Definitely an opportunity. The killer had hidden under Slabov's sister's front porch. Pretty damning. But what about his motive? As far as I knew, he wasn't a witch, a poacher, or a friend of Dobie's. But he might be a friend of Rolaine's. Both his sisters were. What if P.D. was the mysterious lover Rolaine had mentioned? What if he wanted to marry her? Dobie hadn't believed in divorce, and might have made things difficult. With Dobie dead of snakebite, Stu might surface as a serious rival, even if Rolaine believed he wasn't interested. If P.D. had tried to drown LeFever, why wouldn't he be willing to shoot a second rival? It made sense, but not a whole lot.

Of course, Rolaine might have lied to me about a few things. Perhaps Dobie had been right and his wife and Stu had been sleeping together. Stu and Rolaine might have tried to kill her husband by drowning him. And when that didn't work, they might have cooked up the snakebite accident. That would have left the widow with a nice, profitable used car business and an empty spot in her bed for Slaughter.

But then why would Rolaine put suspicion on Stu by cooking up the fishy autopsy story, assuming the college student informant was her invention?

Maybe Rolaine was a double crosser. She might have wanted Stu out of the picture. Was she afraid of her feelings for him? Did she feel she couldn't commit to Slabov as long as Slaughter was still around? Did she talk Slabov into shooting Stu? What if Slaughter had helped poison Dobie, but then decided he couldn't live with his actions and decided to confess to the cops? If Rolaine had been involved, Stu would likely reveal her part in Dobie's murder.

What a mess. My head hurt, and I still really knew nothing.

When I pulled up in front of Rocko's the morning sun was hitting the front window and the blinds were down. I got out of the Nash and went inside.

"How's my little Sweet Potato Strudel?" Tracy greeted me. "How'd things go with the girls last night? Make any conquests?"

"How could I even look at another woman when I've got you, my little Honey Glazed Ham?"

"Stop being nice. You'll make me suspicious."

"Nothing happened last night."

"Oh, yeah? Then why haven't you shaved? Just get back in town?"

"It's a disguise. I'm trying to look tough. I'm on a case, remember?"

"You look like Freddy the Freeloader."

"I was hoping more for a San Fernando Red look."

"Keep working on it."

"I'm hungry. Are the eggs still in the chickens?"

"No. Cookie squeezed them out hours ago. How about an omelet?"

"Too fancy. Fried eggs, toast, bacon or sausage, as long as it's not cat. And coffee."

I decided to throw a scare into Tracy. When she turned her back to shout my order to Cookie, I took the glass eye out of my pocket and set it on the counter. She turned back around.

"'Here's looking at you, Kid,'" she said, in a very bad Bogart impersonation. It sounded more like Sidney Greenstreet. "Is that the private eye I keep hearing about?"

"Damn it, Tracy, doesn't anything ever scare you?"

"The thought that you're my boyfriend makes my teeth chatter."

"I love it when your teeth chatter. This eye likely belonged to the man who was shot in Topaz Canyon the other morning. Somebody sent it to me in the mail."

"Oh, did I miss your birthday?"

"No. I don't know how to take it. Is it a threat, a clue? What?"

"Maybe a practical joke of some kind. I had an uncle, who — "

"I don't want to hear about any more of your relatives. I just met your parents, remember?"

"Hey, watch your mouth. Mom's OK. We go out and do stuff together sometimes. Pop's the black sheep. Drink your coffee, it's getting cold. That makes the grease rise to the top."

My breakfast was ready. I ate it. Cookie's culinary skills hadn't improved any.

"You know, Tracy, I'm just trying to pick up some dough so you and I can go to the carnival."

"I know. But hurry up with it, will you? And stay away from the dames."

"I'll do my best."

I went out to the car and opened the driver's door. There was a rattlesnake coiled up asleep on the passenger's seat. I hurried back into Rocko's.

"Tracy! There's a live rattlesnake in my car."

"Kill it. We'll put it in the chili."

I borrowed a long-handled spatula, and coaxed the snake into a cardboard box that cans of lard had come in. Then I hastily closed up the box and put it on the back seat. I knew just exactly where to take the snake.

I'd heard that Flinders College had adopted Slaughter's snakes, but I wanted to give my little pal his freedom. There was an area a few miles south of town that was mostly desert. Sandstone rock formations, pinion pines, and pear cactus. It was a peaceful, scenic, spot, and good rattlesnake country. I put the box on its side on the ground and opened it. Junior slithered out onto the sand and disappeared into a stand of scrub oak.

First a glass eye, now a rattler. What next? I couldn't stop thinking about it. Somebody was trying to warn me, or scare me, or send me a message. I just wanted them to leave me alone.

I started to think about the case again. If Slabov hadn't killed Stu, then who had? His sister, Ann? She knew how to shoot. She likely felt misused by Stu. She'd had the day off and may or may not have gone to church. She might have used LeFever's death as a convenient time to kill her former lover. But somehow I couldn't see the mother of two sweet little girls gunning down a man in cold blood. I knew there were such women, but I didn't think Ann was that sort. Charlotte had an alibi.

What about Travis Spencer? I disliked the guy enough to want to believe he'd killed Slaughter and would be sent up for it. And according to Bram Duckers, Travis had a motive and had threatened to kill Stu. Used car lots are closed on Sundays, so he'd had the opportunity. But though I could see how Ann would have gotten hold of her brother's rifle, it didn't seem likely that Travis had even known about the gun.

But if Travis had been planning the murder for a time, he could have been prowling parking lots looking for a gun that, for some unaccountable reason, people leave in their vehicles. It was possible he'd been a customer at Vision Quest at one time. His job at the used car lot would have given him the opportunity to learn how to jimmy locked cars. And what about that rock crystal I'd found in back of Charlotte's house? Spencer, or whoever the killer was, might have left that as a plant to put suspicion on Slabov.

None of this added up all that convincingly, but I still thought a visit to Spencer might be a good idea. I could feel him out a little. Besides, I liked the idea of showing up in the Nash and pushing his nose in it a little.

15

When I drove onto the main lot of LeFever's Used Car Gems, Travis was leaning up against the service island, talking through the window with a pretty girl, the same Misty he'd brought over to my office. When he saw me, or rather, my car, he hurried over. He was a big guy all right. Tall, broad, with no fat in sight. I guessed his age at around thirty.

"Why don't you wash this car?" he greeted me. His usual phony smile was nowhere in evidence. "Is that the way you treat your own car? By the way, when are you getting it back from the garage?"

"I think they're still working on the windshield wipers."

"Good thing for you the widow's a pushover. I wouldn't let you keep this beauty one more minute if it was up to me."

"Keep your shirt on, pal. You'll get your precious Ambassador back soon enough. And I'm sure Mrs. LeFever will come up with a special price just for you." I was out of the car now, standing no more than five feet from Travis. "I just came by to give you my condolences. I understand an old hunting buddy of yours was shot to death the other day."

He gave me a sour, puzzled, look. "That Slaughter guy? That jerk was no friend of mine."

"No? Perhaps I was misinformed. I'd heard you'd gone on a hunting trip, maybe in the wrong season, in Topaz Canyon, and Slaughter had something to do with it. Was my informant wrong?"

"Your informant's crazy! And if I find out who he is, I'll beat him into a bloody pancake."

"Now, that's not friendly. You shouldn't threaten folks that way. Especially since you ditched that thirty-caliber carbine you borrowed."

"What?" He took a couple of steps toward me and balled his fists.

I hit him with a quick right. I put everything I had into it. My fist, my arm, my shoulder, my gut, my hips. I hit him where his belly was supposed to be, but somebody had replaced it with a washboard. He grunted, turned red, and folded like a jack knife. He stood there, bent over, and shared his breakfast with the pavement.

"You shouldn't be such a tough guy," I told him. "It's going to get you in trouble." I got into my car and left. My hand felt like I'd punched a meat locker.

My little encounter with Travis had really accomplished nothing. It had been fairly satisfying though. I still had no idea if Spencer had killed Stu. Or if he'd tried to drown Dobie. I hoped my next interview with him would be more informative, and less violent. I stopped to gas up the car. While the attendant was scrubbing my windshield I used a payphone to put in a call to Charlotte at the library. She was in. I told her I'd like to have a little chat with her. She said she was eating her lunch at her desk and to come on by. I drove straight over there.

The public library was a gloomy old stone building, two-storied, near the center of town. It had high ceilings, arched windows, and smelled of dusty books. A fussy-looking guy in a tweed jacket and a bow tie directed me to Charlotte's office. I knocked on the partly-open door and her voice told me to come in. Her smile was nice, but there were dark smudges under her eyes and she had a limp, lank, appearance. I remembered the cocktails she, Ann, and Rolaine had consumed the night before. Likely Charlotte was hung over. Then again, maybe Stu's death was really getting to her. She was eating chicken salad with halved red grapes in it from a Tupperware container, and clattering away at a typewriter on her big metal desk.

"To what do I owe the honor of this visit?" She glanced at me, but went on typing.

"Oh, I don't know. Maybe I just stopped by to

- leer at your legs."

leer at your legs."

"Go ahead and leer. But no drooling. The janitor hates that."

"Actually, I came by to talk about murder and mayhem."

"Have you tracked down Stu's killer yet?"

"No. But I'm narrowing the field. You may not like the list of suspects I've put together."

"I can't be on that list. I have an iron-clad alibi."

"I realize that. But not all of your family members are in that enviable position."

She kept typing, but turned and gave me a quick stare.

"Don't you have a secretary for that?" I asked, pointing at her typewriter.

"Are you kidding? This is a library; we're all expected to type. The only one with a secretary is the director. But I get the hint." She stopped clattering the keys and gave me her full attention. "Listen, about last night, I was kidding when I suggested that Ann might have killed Stu. I was just reacting to too much gin."

"I know that. I didn't need you to give me the idea that either Ann, or P.D., could have committed the crime. Don't get mad at me. The cops will likely come to the same conclusions I have. Neither your brother nor your sister have solid alibis, unless Ann really went to church that morning, and your brother was actually working by himself in his optical shop. However, there's something else you need to know: it was your brother's rifle

158

that killed Stu. That's practically been proven. And he can't account for his whereabouts at the time of the shooting. I learned last night that Ann and P.D. went hunting together in their younger days. So, they both know how to shoot."

"My siblings aren't killers." Her nostrils were beginning to flare. "Why would either of them do such a thing, even if they were capable of it?"

"Revenge. Jealousy. I don't know the reasons. I'm going to ask you a question, and I hope you'll answer it. I'll find out anyway, it'll just take me longer. And if you don't talk to me, the time will come when you'll have to talk to the cops."

"Ask your question."

"Rolaine was cheating on her husband. That's none of my business, but the identity of her lover might be my business. You probably know who the guy is. I'm going to throw out some names. The first name is Philo Dexter Slabov. Is he Rolaine's lover?"

She was silent for a moment. She even gazed longingly at her sturdy Royal typewriter. "Is he a suspect? I mean, are the police interested in him?"

"Yes. Like I said, it was his rifle that killed Stu. He reported it stolen after the murder."

"Anybody could have taken that gun. He's kept it in his Jeep for years."

"Granted. But if he's involved with Dobie's wife, and he considered Stu a possible rival — "

Charlotte laughed, but it was a bitter sound.

"I don't think P.D. has the passion for that kind

of crime. Besides, he's a pretty confidant man. Why wouldn't he think he could hold his own against a rival, without killing him?"

I shrugged. "I can't explain such things."

"Ann, on the other hand, is too passionate. She always thinks whatever new man she picks up is going to be the one and only. She pesters them, dogs them, drives them crazy with her demands and expectations. And then she wonders why they leave her. She might have had fantasies about killing Stu, but I can't believe she'd actually do such a thing."

"I see. Getting back to P.D., is he Rolaine's lover or not?"

"If he is, it's not for me to tell you. I'd be giving away someone else's secrets."

"Somebody else said something like that to me recently."

"Who?"

"My lips are sealed. Just like yours."

"Don't you have any other suspects?"

"Sure, but nobody you're acquainted with. Thanks for your time."

I was thinking of driving up to Topaz Canyon again to talk to Rolaine. I didn't know what would come of it, but I couldn't think of what else to do. I decided to stop off at my office first. Who knew, maybe the phone would ring.

I sat at my desk, playing with the very same pencil Dobie had played with when he'd come to me for help. I sure hadn't helped him any. I had four suspects, and I hadn't yet looked into the witch angle. I'd have to go back to Soupy's to talk to Eldon Sponk. The phone rang. It was Bram Duckers. He had another suspect for me.

"I've been looking into the Slaughter slaying," Bram told me. He liked to talk that way. "I thought it was the least I could do for not telling you about my being a poacher."

"Forget about that. Just keep your nose clean in the future."

"I even took a day off to help you. Celeste is about to kill me. She keeps talking about the expense of baby formula and diapers, but the kid's not even born yet! Anyhow, I have a name. Royal Grimpin. Goes by Roy. Owns a car dealership over in Wavering Haze. Sells Buicks. Single, pretty much married to his work. He's one of those guys who can't forget about the war. You know the type. Twenty years from now he'll still be boring people with his war stories. The best time of his life. Why don't guys like him stay in the military if they liked it so much?"

"Couldn't tell you. What about this Roy?"

"He was a good friend of Mr. LeFever's. And he was a hunter. I think he might have hired Slaughter as a guide at some point. Anyhow, from what I could find out, he's pretty broken up about the death of his friend. LeFever and him were partners at one time, years ago. LeFever bought-out Grimpin's part of the business when Grimpin decided to start the Buick dealership.

"Grimpin drove over to Quartz Quarry two days after the snakebite accident. Wanted to make sure he didn't miss the funeral. Wanted to be a shoulder to cry on if Mrs. LeFever was so inclined. He's still in town, staying at Gurdy Perkins' Heaven's Haven Motel. Says he's staying until after Slaughter's funeral. Wants to attend it. This guy loves military guns. Do you know what kind of gun Slaughter was killed with?"

"A military one. An M1 Carbine. But the cops have the murder weapon, and it wasn't owned by this Royal Grimpin. Still, he might be a pretty good shot with one. You talk to this guy?"

"Some. Not much. I didn't want him to get his feathers ruffled and maybe start covering his tracks. I wanted to talk to you before I did anything else on my own."

"I owe you. I hope you've kept track of the hours you've put in."

"Skip it. It's on me. That guy, if you want to talk to him, is staying in number one-oh-two. I saw him today, but he was talking about going up to see the widow."

"Today? When did you talk to him?"

"No more than a couple of hours ago."

"I was getting ready to head up to the widow's myself. You got anything else? Has Grimpin talked to anyone, maybe in a bar, about wanting to kill anybody?"

"Not that I've found out. Grimpin's a tea teetotaler. Like I said, married to his job."

162

"Thanks, Bram. I appreciate it. I'll get back to you. Wait, how'd you hear about this Grimpin?"

"He was at the shooting range. He's a talker. Blubbered like a baby when somebody mentioned seeing something in the papers about the rattler killing."

"Rattler killing. This guy was at the range to shoot, I take it. What was he shooting?"

"Wasn't a rifle. Some big revolver. Not American. A Webbley. British."

"Good shot?"

"Tack driver, when he wasn't crying."

I drove up to Rolaine's. I figured with any luck Grimpin might still be there. If not, I could talk to Rolaine about him. It was a cool September day and I enjoyed the drive.

When I reached the widow's, a big Buick ragtop was parked there with the top down. I glanced in at the dashboard as I headed for the house. All the bells and whistles. The car looked like it'd just been washed. How that could be with all the dust in the air I couldn't imagine. Maybe Grimpin, because it had to be him, had driven five miles an hour.

16

Rolaine answered my knock and let me in. She was wearing her favorite outfit of jeans, saddle shoes, and a man's shirt. The shirt was red and went well with her black hair and her almost olive complexion, but she looked strained and a little washed out.

"Axe, I'm glad you're here. I have a visitor. An old friend of my husband's. Come meet him. I'll put coffee on."

She led me into the living room. A man was sitting on the couch next to the coffee table. He stood up and shook hands with me. He was short, fat, and sweaty. He wore a too-tight gray suit, a white shirt, and a red tie that all looked like it was strangling him. His too-long hair was plastered all over his head like he'd just gotten out of the pool.

"I'm Roy," he told me. "Friend of Dobie's. Are you a friend of Dobie's? Don't remember seeing you at the funeral."

"I was busy. Axe Hatchett. Nice to meet you."

"Mr. Hatchett is investigating my husband's death," said Rolaine. "He's a private investigator. He's also looking into the shooting of Mr. Slaughter."

"Guy had it coming to him," said Roy, with no attempt to conceal his dislike of Slaughter. "Funeral's day after tomorrow, when the lab boys get through with him. Boy, am I going to enjoy that."

"You like funerals, Roy?" I asked.

"As a general rule, no. This funeral I'm going to love. What kind of a guy keeps snakes in the garage? I'm telling you, it ought to be a crime. Might as well have put a gun to Dobie's head, or gotten drunk and run him down with a car."

He turned on the waterworks. Between his sweating and his crying, Roy was putting out a whole lot of water. I hoped he wouldn't flood the place. He took out a checked hanky the size and color of a tablecloth in an Italian restaurant and started mopping off some of the moisture.

"Excuse me," he wailed, in a broken voice. "Excuse me. That Dobie, he was salt of the earth. What a guy. Salt of the earth. Pepper of the earth, for that matter. Can't say enough about him. The world will miss him."

"Of course," I said. "He was a swell guy. Who didn't like him? Now, Slaughter, that's a different matter, isn't it? Who wouldn't have wanted to kill him for what he did?"

"I tell you, buddy," he stuck a pudgy finger at me, "if somebody else hadn't gotten to him first,

I'd a done it."

"Watch what you're saying. I mean, we all think about those things, killing bad people, but doing it's different."

"I'm trained. Were you in the service?"

"Two years in the Army."

"See any action?"

"I peeled some pretty mean spuds doing KP."

"Oh, you're being modest. You're being modest. I can tell by looking at your face, you saw some action. Saw some blood. Were you a sergeant? I'll bet you were a sergeant."

"Let's just say I never won enough stripes to upholster a zebra."

"But you had three, right? You had three stripes?"

"That was a long time ago. A lot of water under the bridge. What about you? See a lot of action? I bet you were a general."

"Huh? Buck private. That was me. I was stationed in Memphis the whole two years. Never even got a look at the enemy. But I was ready. I was just waiting to get shipped out to some God-awful place. Never happened. Some things you can't fix. Hey, do you remember the food? Chipped beef? That awful gray mutton? Powdered eggs? Torture. Eating in the Army was torture."

"So, you never actually shot anybody?"

"Don't rub it in. That's not nice. No, I never killed anybody. But I was ready, I was trained."

"But that doesn't mean you could actually kill someone. I mean, did you plan it out? Shooting Slaughter?"

"Does that bother you? I planned it out, even drove up to his house. Rolaine here had to show me the way. And I went target practicing. If some other guy hadn't done it, I would of. Believe you me. Dobie and me were like this." He crossed two of his fat fingers, shook them at me. His glasses fell off his face and onto the rug. He reached down and retrieved them, grunting. "Happens all the time," he laughed. "Sometimes I sit on them. I'm all the time taking them in someplace to get them adjusted, straightened out. Happens all the time. You a friend of Dobie's? Did I already ask you that?"

Rolaine came in from the kitchen, bringing me a cup of coffee on a tray along with a plate of cookies. She set the tray down on the coffee table, and I saw there was a second plate, with one cookie and a bunch of crumbs. Amazingly, Grimpin was crying into his table cloth again. The guy could have washed his car with the amount of moisture he put out.

"More lemonade, Mr. Grimpin?" Rolaine asked.

"Ah, please, call me Roy. I feel like we're family, you and me. Me and your husband was that close. But, honestly, I ought to get going. I've taken up too much of your time. And you've got your detective here. I'm sure you two need to talk." He stood up, turned to me. "If you find the guy who killed Slaughter, let me know. I'll give him a free Buick. I mean it, a Buick. Nice meeting you."

"Thanks for coming by," Rolaine said. "And thanks for rescuing me."

"Huh? That was nothing, just nothing. Tough break you got that disease. Hope you get over it."

She maneuvered him to the door and got him through it. In a minute I heard the big Buick start up.

"I thought he'd never leave," Rolaine told me, when she came back to the living room and sat down in the spot Roy had just vacated. "I shouldn't be ungrateful, but the man is such a bore."

"What kind of rescue were you talking about?"

"I was outside when Roy arrived. I'd gone out into the garden because I wanted to try it on my own. I don't want to be dependent on other people any longer. But I couldn't do it. I didn't get any farther than the bottom of the steps. I froze there, hanging onto the railing. I don't know how long I was out there. Roy drove up. I heard a car but I couldn't do anything; I couldn't move. I called for help though. It was awful. He came around the house and into the garden and I had to explain things to him. He helped me into the house. He treated me like a child. But it wasn't his fault. He was actually being kind. Who knows how long I would have been out there if he hadn't come along. I guess until you showed up. I'd rather have been rescued by you."

"I think you're going to need Charlotte's help for a while longer. That's my guess. But you'll get there; you'll get better. Tell me about this Roy guy. He and your husband used to work together, I gather. They must have been really good friends."

"Roy thinks so.

"Your husband wasn't so sure?"

"No. He thought Roy was a bore, just like I do. He was glad when Roy offered to sell his share of the business."

"And this is the guy who was willing to murder Stu for the sake of revenge. But you don't think he really did it?"

"I doubt it. When I first saw him, two days after Dobie's death, he didn't say anything about revenge. He wanted to see Stu's place, but he didn't say why. When he called me this morning, and said he might drop by again sometime, he was full of blood and thunder. A big talker. I don't think he'd kill anyone."

"I'm inclined to agree. When it comes to his murderous intentions, he's what my neighbor, Blythe, would call, 'all hat and no cattle.' Still, he might have done it. It's worth looking into. By the way, why didn't you mention this Grimpin character to me earlier?"

"Maybe I forgot. I probably pushed his visit to the back of my mind. Besides, as I just told you, he didn't mention anything about avenging Dobie's death that time. Or later at the funeral."

"OK."

She seemed nervous, or restless. Her eyes kept moving over to the hassock, which had been moved to the end of the couch since my last visit. There was a cardboard box sitting on it. She saw me looking.

"Dobie's personal affects. From the undertakers. The police had them before that. Charlotte picked them up for me and dropped them off yesterday."

"Mind if I look? Or am I being unnecessarily nosey?"

"Go ahead and look."

I got up from my chair and went over to the box. I took inventory. Some keys on a leather key fob. A wallet, some loose change. A comb and handkerchief. A second hanky, a lady's. That caught my eye. It was crumpled and looked well used. I picked it up. There was a monogram in one corner. "A.H." I glanced at Rolaine.

"Smell it."

I took a sniff. "Perfume."

"Perfume. And cigarette smoke. And the dirty fingers of a used car dealer. The initials stand for Ann Hepple. Charlotte's sister."

"You don't think — ? I mean, your husband could have found the hanky on the ground, the floor. He picked it up and put it in his pocket and forgot about it."

She shook her head. "I don't think so. It's been handled too much, like a memento. It meant something to him. No doubt he carried it with him to remind him of her. He'd take it out of his pocket now and then to sniff it. Like a dog."

"Are you sure about this? Have you talked to Ann?"

"I don't care if I ever speak to her again. I told you that Dobie had his occasional flings. But this one must have meant something to him."

"Don't jump to conclusions."

"I'll do what I damned well please."

"Sure. That's fine. I can see you're upset. Tell me, you knew your husband had affairs, but you didn't seem much bothered by them. What makes this encounter with Ann different?"

"Because I thought Ann was my friend, and now I find out she was sleeping with my husband behind my back. And something else. The way that handkerchief had been handled, and cherished, and carried around. That means Dobie actually cared about Ann. Most of the time he just slept with women. He didn't actually care about them. I know my own behavior has been bad, so I really shouldn't feel anything at all about Dobie's sleeping with Ann, but I do."

"All right. I can understand how you'd feel betrayed by Ann. Listen, I need to get back to town. I think you could use some time by yourself."

An ugly thought was forming in the back of my mind, and it wasn't good news for Ann. I got away from Rolaine's house as quickly as decent manners would allow. I had a couple of pretty important things to do. The first was to visit Charlotte's house. The next was to call Charlotte.

A misty rain was beginning to fall as I parked my car in front of Charlotte's place. Her little Jeepster was not in the drive, so I figured she must still be at the library. I got out and walked around the outside of the house. The stone foundation was about two-and-a-half feet high. Assuming the crawlspace was dug out a little, a person, man or woman, could probably crawl under the house on hands and knees. Even a big guy like Travis Spencer could alligator crawl from the crawlspace door in back to under the front porch. The little door was just big enough to admit a good-sized man.

But was it big enough to allow the passage of a rotund number like Roy Grimpin? I doubted it. But he made a nice suspect in some ways. Friend of Dobie's — at least he thought so — familiar with guns, mouthy about wanting to kill Stu. Even the fact that he wore glasses and liked to sit on them. He might have bent up his specs while he was staying at the motel. He could have asked directions to the nearest optical shop. From Heaven's Haven that was likely Vision Quest. He could have noticed Slabov's Jeep in the parking lot and gone over to look at it. He liked military stuff. If he'd looked in the back seat he might have seen the folded up rifle on the floor, which would provide him with a murder weapon that couldn't be traced to him. He was staying alone in the motel, likely keeping to himself. It all added up pretty good. But I still wasn't certain he could stuff his portly self through Charlotte's house's crawlspace entrance.

When I hit town. I stopped at the first pay-phone I found and called the library. Charlotte was still there. I talked to her and said I was on my way over to talk about something that couldn't wait but couldn't be discussed over the phone. I wanted to see her in person.

"You have a crush on me, don't you?" she said, over the phone, with a laugh in her voice.

"It's those freckles; I can't get enough of them. Besides, I haven't counted them all yet. Listen, I'll be over in a few minutes."

"I'm getting ready to leave. I've had enough of the library for one day. I'll meet you out front. There's a bench under a big tree near the front entrance."

At the library, I slipped the Nash into a slot next to Charlotte's yellow chariot. I found her where she'd said she'd be. She had some kind of satchel, stuffed with books, on the bench beside her, and was watching a sparrow getting cleaned up for a date in a birdbath a few yards away. She was smiling when I approached, but the smile faded as she took in my no doubt grim face.

"What is it?" she asked, as I sat down next to her, the satchel between us.

"First of all, I might have good news. It's possible I've stumbled across the guy who killed Slaughter, and it's not P.D. However, there are some questions. I'll keep my eye on the guy. Listen, try this on for size, and please don't be secretive. That won't help anyone. "

"Shoot me the pill."

"Where'd you pick that up? Do you think it's possible Ann and Dobie were lovers?"

She gave it some thought. "With Ann, who knows? Yes, I think it's possible."

"There's some evidence. If Ann and Dobie were lovers, given her personality, that might give her a pretty strong motive for killing Stu. That would make Stu not just the guy who jilted her, but the guy who killed her current lover, perhaps on purpose. How's that sound?"

"Truthfully? If Ann's capable of murder, that combination might give her reason enough. Do the police know about this?"

"No, and they aren't likely to figure it out. But if your sister murdered Stu Slaughter, then she has to get sent up for it, even if she goes to the gas chamber. I'm sorry, but that's how it is."

"Do you really think you have enough evidence to prove she killed Stu?"

"No, I don't. I could use some help."

"You want me to help you convict my sister of murder?"

"I want you to do what's right. If you don't cooperate, I'll understand. But I'll still get the evidence I need, if it exists."

She picked up a maple leaf that had fallen onto the bench from the tree overhead and started twirling it around by its stem.

"If I help you — Ann needs to confess. I won't believe my sister killed anyone unless she confesses to it."

"She has to confess. If she doesn't, she might get away with it. But, you know what? In that case the cops may go after your brother."

"You're trying to twist my arm."

"All I'm doing is telling you the truth as I understand it."

"I'd like to invite you to dinner at my house."

"Because I'm such a swell guy?"

"Not just you. Ann, P.D., Rolaine. Maybe we can trick Ann into confessing, if she's guilty. I want some time to think about this."

"I can give you a little. Not much. When do you want to have this dinner?"

She shook her head slowly. "I'll let you know. Give me your phone number."

I dug out one of my cards and gave it to her. It had both my office and home phone numbers on it.

"You realize," she said, "that if Ann did this, she set up P.D. She stole his rifle."

"Yeah, but she hid it afterwards. What bothers me is the rock."

"What rock?"

"A nice Amazonite crystal I found in the mud in back of your house the morning Stu was shot. It's likely the same stone your brother had in his Jeep."

"Why would Ann, or anyone, leave it at the

scene?"

"Good question. Maybe as a plant to frame him. And he's a known rock hound. Still, you're right. As a plant, it stinks. Maybe the killer just took the rock because it's pretty, stuck it in his pocket, and it fell out while he, or she, was navigating your crawlspace door."

"It gives me the screaming meemies — is that from the war? — just to think of Stu's murderer slithering under my house. I hope it wasn't Ann, but I'll help you. I'll tell you when I'm ready for the dinner."

"Thanks. I'm with you, Charlotte — I really hope it wasn't Ann who killed Stu. But it doesn't look good. I'm just full of good news, aren't I?"

"You've got an odd way of wooing a girl."

"What girl wants to be wooed by little old me? I'm a plug-ugly gumshoe with bad manners and a gut."

"You have a certain deeply-buried charm."

"Stop your flattery. Who knows? Maybe your sister really did go to church that day. If so, there's bound to be someone who saw her there."

"I don't think she went to church. I think she went to some lovers' lair. It's the way she's been acting. She's got a new boyfriend. But if she was Dobie's lover, you're right, she might have gone to church."

17

I left Charlotte sitting on her bench and headed home. When I got there I called Bram at the Happy Trails Shooting Range. He wasn't there. I tried his home. Celeste answered and grudgingly turned the phone over to her husband.

"Bram? Listen. You might be right about Grimpin. Here's what I want you to do, and keep track of your hours. Slaughter's funeral is the day after tomorrow. Check the obits, or call around to the funeral homes. Find out when the funeral is.

"Don't attend it. That might make you look like a friend of Slaughter. Park out front of the cemetery. I'm sure you know what kind of car Grimpin drives — a big Buick ragtop. Follow him after the funeral. If he goes to a restaurant or something, you go there too. If he goes back to the motel, or heads for Wavering Haze, follow him. Arrange an accidental meeting. I know the guy doesn't drink, and that's too bad. Get him talking; that's easy enough. Buy him a sody pop and a pizza, or a hot roast beef sandwich. Get him stirred up. Get him bawling. If he killed Slaughter, I want you to dig a confession out of him. He might be suspicious of you. It could take a light touch, or a really heavy one. Are you up to it?"

"You can count on me. For real."

"Good boy. Call me when you've got something. And don't forget to add gas and food to your expenses."

I fried up a can of Spam, added a fried egg, and called it supper. Then I put on my tough guy clothes and headed for Soupy's Rot Gut Bucket. I didn't expect to find out much, but it was worth a shot. I left the Nash in a well-lighted parking lot several blocks north of Soupy's. The neighborhood was marginally better than his. Now that it was night, there were a lot more people on the streets. I walked among panhandlers, pimps, and prostitutes, polite folks for the most part.

Soupy's door was still hanging open, and a lot of noise was coming out of the place. Inside the dimly-lit dive a beat-up juke box was pouring out the sad story of some dame's cheating heart, and how it was going to tell on her. Poor kid. Guys built like stevedores, with mashed-in faces, were playing pool, ready to turn their cue sticks into clubs at a moment's notice. Some more guys were playing cards at the round tables crowded onto the floor.

Some ladies were present, some unattached for now. They wore a lot of makeup, fancy hairdos, and not an excessive amount of clothes. I grabbed a stool at the bar among a crew of stalwart gents and showy damsels. The bartender was an eyeful. He was average height, short in the leg, with the upper body contours of a weight lifting orangutan. His arms showed some tattoos. Skulls and daggers, shapely maidens, and "Mom" in quaint lettering. His face was that of a fairly content Buddha. I guessed this was Eldon Sponk. He was waiting tables when I came in, carrying a tray as big around as a tractor tire. When he returned to the bar he gave me a little of his attention.

"What'll it be, bud?"

I'd learned my lesson from the morning. He wouldn't like me ordering coffee.

"Rye, with a beer chaser." What the hell, I hadn't had a drink in months. I was likely on the verge of solving a murder case. A bit of celebrating wouldn't hurt.

He poured my rye, drew my beer, and shoved both beverages in my direction. An aging girl slid not too gracefully onto the stool next to mine.

"How about buying me a drink, dream boat? My Name's Amber. Amber Divine."

Sure it is, I thought. "I don't speak English."

"You're speaking it."

"I'm deaf and dumb."

"Dumb maybe, but you can hear."

"Pay day's a long way down the road."

She heard that. "I'll come back when you're drunker. Maybe some generosity will kick in." She slid back off the stool and went trolling elsewhere.

I turned my attention to the libations. I sniffed the rye. It stank like something you'd use to remove stubborn barnacles off the bottom of a boat. I tasted it. It made me feel sorry for the barnacles. I finished it and chased it with the beer. I hoped it would catch up in a hurry. Eldon was busy filling orders along the bar. When he finally came back my way I signaled for refills. He brought them.

"I'm looking for Eldon Sponk."

"Lucky you. I'm him."

"I've got some questions for you."

"I got an answer for all of them. It starts with 'N' and ends with 'O', and there ain't no letters in between."

"Don't be like that. I'm a guy who's writing a book."

"That so? I read one once. Had a bunch of phone numbers in it."

"It's about witches."

"Sure it is."

"I'm looking for a different slant, a gimmick. There's been plenty of books written about witches. I don't want to write the same old thing."

"How about you don't write nothing?"

"Naw, that wouldn't pay. Somebody gave me your name."

"Really? Your name's Eldon?"

"No. This somebody said you were a pretty interesting guy. Said you might be a witch."

"They call them warlocks. I ain't one of them.

Knew a dizzy dame once that was a witch. Kind of a looker. I fell for her."

"Did it work out for you, if you know what I mean?"

"Not so much. Took me on a picnic out in the woods. At midnight. Bunch of witches out there. We all danced around in our long johns. Only we wasn't wearing any. Sound like fun?"

"Sure. I've heard they do that."

"Wasn't a whole lot of fun. Buddy, some of those witch frails should keep their clothes on even when they're taking baths. To make things worse, a couple of them warlocks showed up. Who wants to see a naked guy? It was like being back in the Navy."

The conversation was going a lot better than I could have hoped. I downed my second rye and my second beer, and ordered more. Eldon brought me more drinks. Then he went up and down the bar and offered refills. One of the card players yelled something from one of the tables. Eldon loaded up his tray again, hoisted it into the air, and carried it to his thirsty customers. When he got back he started talking to me again.

"Where were we?" he asked.

I sampled my third rye. It tasted better than the first two. I guess because it was older.

"We were talking about witches and warlocks jigging without their skivvies."

"Right. Who told you about me? About my capering with them naked dames?"

"I can't tell you. There's such a thing as confidentiality."

"And there's such a thing as a big fat fist."

"That's a good point. But, hey, I don't want to get anyone in trouble."

He leaned over the bar. His breath smelled liked Life Savers. Dead-cat-flavored Life Savers. "Tell me."

"A broad named Ann. Don't know the last name. Kind of cute."

Eldon laughed. At least, I think that's what he did. It could have been a yodel blown through a kazoo.

"Her. Yeah. She's the dame. That's the one I fell for. Listen, there ain't nothing wrong with what she's got under her duds. No sirree."

"How'd the night end for you?"

He scowled. Not a pretty sight. "Guy came out of nowhere. Had a flashlight and a gun. Busted up the party. Sent us all home without our clothes. And I'd been wearing my favorite shirt. The one with the sweat stains under the armpits. If that guy hadn't been carrying a gun, I'd of busted him one good. But you know what? Funny thing. A few months later the same guy came into this bar, came into Soupy's. But he didn't have his gun with him."

"What about the flashlight?"

"Who cares about the flashlight?

I finished my drinks and Eldon kindly replenished them.

"Hey, you going to pay for all that?"

I got out my wallet and dug out some bills and handed them too him. He didn't give me change.

"I laid into that guy, but he didn't want to fight. Said he had a bad back. I figured he was yellow, so I kept hitting him. Then he started hitting back." He shook his head back and forth like a mule that's enjoying its work. "He give me this scar."

He pointed at his face. The scar he pointed at shared parking space with about twenty others.

"Thought the guy was going to kill me. Me, Eldon Sponk. Wiped up the floor with me. Put me in the hospital. Funny thing, though. You'll laugh at this. The guy had a glass eye. I got in an extra good punch and that eye popped out and hit the floor. I thought I was going to faint. And I don't faint easy."

"Did you ever catch the guy's name?"

"He might have thrown it. Maybe Butcher or something."

"Slaughter?"

"Yeah. Hey, how do you know?"

"I met him. He told me about the fight, but he didn't say it was in Soupy's. You'll be happy to hear the guy's dead. Got shot to death. Hey, can I get another rye? A double. Skip the chaser."

He brought me back a bigger glass, filled to the brim. Then he went along the bar and took orders. The card table gang sang out, so he grabbed his tray again. When he got back to me I couldn't quite remember what we'd been talking about. I took a sip of rye. Good stuff. Top shelf.

"Hey," said Eldon, "I ain't happy that guy's dead. Hell, he was my friend."

"How do you figure?"

"A fight like that always makes you friends. Damn, that's bad news. Look what you done now. Made me sad. Finish your drink and get out of here."

I finished my drink. I paid for it and was about to leave. A floozy came up to me. A very big floozy. Around two-hundred-and-fifty pounds, but a good ten pounds of that was face paint. She didn't look happy. She grabbed my coat collar and shook me.

"Hey, what'd you say to my friend, Amber? You made her cry."

"I told her I didn't have any dough."

"And here you've been drinking like a prince, and standing drinks for everybody at the bar, no doubt. You got money."

"I didn't stand anybody any drinks. Listen — "

"You're a stinking louse." She gave me a shove. I danced backwards a couple of steps. My coat flew open and the floozy must have seen my gun.

"What are you, a cop?"

"Just a gumshoe."

"That's even worse. A peeper. I'll show you." She laid into me with a left, a right, a left. I ended up on the sidewalk out front, and somebody threw my hat at me. I got up, but it took a long time. They should keep the sidewalks still at night. This one kept twisting around and hitting me in the face. It finally stopped.

I took my hat and started walking to my car. No, I was going the wrong way. I turned around. No, I was turned around again.

I figured it out at last and headed for the parking lot where I'd parked the Nash. It took a long time. The prostitutes I met looked a lot better than the ones I'd seen on my way to Soupy's. Must have been a different batch.

I got back into my car somehow. My face hurt. My nose was bleeding, and I'd scraped my palms on the sidewalk. My gut was queasy and painful. I sat in the car and tried to get a little shuteye. No luck. The moon kept using some power lines for a jump rope. When that finally stopped, I reclined the seat back all the way and closed my eyes.

When I woke up the moon had moved quite a ways, but at least it wasn't skipping rope any longer. I picked my hat off the seat beside me and took a good look at it. Quite a few new creases and dents had been added, but they hadn't improved its appearance. I did my best to restore my fedora to its original splendor, without a lot of success, then I headed home. I wanted my bed.

By the time the Nash finally lurched into my drive, I was feeling a little better. I went inside and applied some cold water to my broken face. I started some coffee, even stronger than usual, and when it was done I drank about half of it. Then I went to bed with my clothes on and fell asleep.

That lasted about five seconds. The phone started ringing. I fumbled my way in the dark to the living room and found the damned phone.

18

"Axe's Hatchett's. No nut too cracked — no, wait."

"Axe, is that really you?"

It was Tracy. I tried to act normal. Tracy didn't cotton to boozing.

"How's my little fruit-fly-infested honeydew?" That sounded pretty good.

"You been drinking, or what?"

"Yeah. I've been hitting the cooking sherry. Sorry. I was on a case."

"You sound funny."

"That's because I'm wearing my clown mask. Why you calling so late? Something happen?"

"It's Pop. Somebody beat him up. I need a ride over to Mom's. You in a condition to drive me?"

"Sure, I'm OK. Just a little muzzy. Somebody beat up your dad? How? When?"

"A couple of hours ago, Mom says. Caught him in the parking lot of Jeremiah's. A big guy. Pop thinks he knows who it was, but it was kind of dark. That parking lot's not lit too well. He won't go to the hospital. What's with you guys and hospitals?"

"We're tough, and we don't like spending money. Let me pour some more coffee down my throat and I'll be right over."

"I'll be standing in front of Rocko's."

I put more cold water on my face, then drank the rest of the coffee. I'd been asleep for such a short time that the coffee was still warm. I crawled into the Nash and headed for Rocko's. Tracy actually lives in a room above the place. When I got there she was standing out in front like promised, wearing a cloth coat and clutching a purse in front of her. She looked like a sad little girl.

"Tell me exactly what happened," I said, as she slid into the passenger seat. "Why would somebody maul your dad? The food at Jeremiah's isn't that bad."

"Pop's still a little confused about it. The guy was some fellow Pop used to go poaching with. Big sap of a used car salesman."

"Travis Spencer?"

"Could be. I don't know the chump. He told Pop he was getting his revenge for Pop's ratting on him about something. And it's your fault. Hey, your face looks worse than usual. Did you fall on it?"

"An Amazon used me for boxing practice. It's a long story; I'll tell you about it later. How's it my fault your dad got attacked?"

"The thug claimed Pop must have been talking to some 'sawed-off, pudgy, peeper.' That's you."

"I'm sorry, Tracy. But it was a different guy who spilled the beans about a poaching incident. Your Pop's innocent."

"Don't do it again."

"What, my job?"

"Be more careful."

"I'm always careful."

"Yeah. You look it. Thanks for dropping me off at Mom's. She's worried. She didn't want to come pick me up because she didn't want to leave Pop alone."

I'd dropped Tracy off at her folks' house a couple of times before, though I'd never been inside their pre-war bungalow. It was in a sleepy part of town.

"You want me to come in with you?"

"No. You smell like a turpentine factory."

"Tell your folks I'm a house painter."

"They already know what you do. I've told them all about you. At least, I've told Mom. I don't talk to Pop much. Don't worry, I didn't bad mouth you behind your back. I only do that to your face. Here we are. Thanks. Go home and get some sleep. Mom will take me home, or I'll grab a cab."

"No. Call me. I'll come pick you up."

"We'll see."

When she stepped out of the car, I could tell she was madder than usual. I wondered if it was because I'd been drinking, or if she really blamed me for her dad's getting beat up. Hell, it wasn't my fault. It was Travis Spencer's. Then I had an idea. I found a drugstore and went inside and used the payphone to call Bram Duckers and warn him. I hoped I wasn't too late. If Spencer had mangled Jerry Clover, he might go after Bram as well. I thought about calling the cops to have the gorilla put in the tank, but if it ended up in the papers, Tracy wouldn't like it.

After about ten rings, Celeste picked up. When she found out who she was talking to her voice went down in temperature about seventy degrees. My hand was getting frostbite just by holding the phone.

"Bram can't talk to you. I'm sure you know why."

"Somebody roughed him up?"

"Yes. They were waiting for him by the garage when he got home. He's hurt, but he won't go to the hospital. I think his nose might be broken. Bram said the beating might have something to do with you."

"I'm sorry, I really am." Bram with a broken nose. That was terrible. It might make him noticeable, ruin his nondescript appearance. "You sure I can't talk to him?"

"I'm sure. He's hurt, he's in bed. Leave him alone."

"Sure, but have him give me a call in the morning."

She hung up on me.

19

It was a couple of days before Charlotte was able to put together her special dinner. That was fine; it gave me time to sober up and heal up. By that time both Bram and Tracy's dad were on the mend. Neither victim chose to involve the police. I guess they were afraid of Spencer's possible retaliation. The guest list for Charlotte's chicken dinner included me, Ann, P.D., and Rolaine. Ernie was to be confined in solitary in Charlotte's bedroom. Ann's kids would stay with Grandma. The show was to start at seven.

I arrived about six-thirty, but I was the last to arrive. Ann's green pickup and P.D.'s Jeep were already parked along the side of the house in Charlotte's yard. I found a piece of pasture for my car and went to the door. A strained-looking Rolaine answered the door and invited me in. The cooking odors made my belly growl. I hoped Ernie wouldn't hear. Everyone was having cocktails. I asked for my usual coffee. I wondered if Ann had any idea what was about to happen. I doubted it.

After drinks, the better to lubricate Ann's tongue, we all sat down at a big table in a room off the kitchen for an old-fashioned Sunday chicken dinner. Only it wasn't Sunday, and none of us was especially old-fashioned. There were two fried chickens, corn on the cob, creamed peas and new potatoes, and the ubiquitous Jell-O salad. There were nice fluffy biscuits, and it was rumored there would be apple pie for dessert.

I was so nervous that I could hardly eat. I noticed that some of the other diners only picked at their food. That was too bad, because Charlotte turned out to be a good cook. Only Ann tucked in like a farmer who's just finished plowing about a hundred acres.

P.D. started the ball rolling. He wasn't a naturally good actor, but he got better as he warmed to his subject.

"I have some disturbing news for all of you. My days of freedom might be nearly over. I'm not sure what I'll do with Vision Quest. Maybe close it."

"What's happened, brother?" Charlotte asked.

Ann said nothing, but concentrated on spearing some peas on her plate with a fork. It seemed to take up all her attention.

"Well," said P.D., sighing — he really was getting better — "I'm part of a murder investigation. In fact, I'm at the center." He turned to me. "Could

I trouble you for another biscuit?"

I passed him the towel-lined basket. He selected a biscuit, cut it open, and slathered butter on it.

"It's all because I kept that damned rifle in my Jeep. I don't know what I was thinking. I guess I believed I might be attacked by a bear or a mountain lion while I was rock hunting." He munched his biscuit slowly. I believe he was beginning to enjoy his performance. "Somebody stole the gun, and I don't even know when that might have been. The police found it, hidden. It'd been fired recently. And here's the worst part. The rifle was used to kill Stu Slaughter, a man I hardly knew. The slug that killed him came from my gun, and the cartridges remaining in the magazine have my fingerprints on them.

"When I discovered the gun missing, I immediately reported it to the police. That was the day after the murder. I, of course, had no idea. It's odd. I wouldn't have noticed the theft if Mr. Waldengarver here — I'm sorry, Mr. Hatchett — hadn't shown up at the shop with an Amazonite crystal that looked exactly like one I'd found in Topaz Canyon a couple of weeks earlier. I'd left it on the passenger's seat of the Jeep. It was something for me to look at when I was stopped in traffic. As soon as I got home the day Mr. Hatchett had called on me, I looked in the Jeep for the stone. It was gone, and so was my rifle.

"Now the police believe that I shot poor Slaughter. And I can't blame them. I'm likely going to prison, or the gallows, or the electric chair, or however they do things in Colorado."

"They gas you with cyanide," I said, helpfully. Rolaine placed her napkin over her mouth and kept it there, but didn't say anything. Now that I thought about it, Rolaine hadn't spoken to, or even looked at, Ann all evening.

"Thank you," said P.D. "If the real killer doesn't come forward, I'm sunk. I have no alibi. I was working in the lab that day, by myself." He turned to me again. "Would you please pass the strawberry jam? I have just this little crumb of biscuit left."

"You know," I said, passing the jam, "that rock crystal business is interesting. Are you sure it's the same one that was in your Jeep? I found it in the mud in back of this very house. I'm feeling kind of guilty. If it wasn't for me, that rifle might never have been found. I discovered its location and reported it to the police. I didn't want to mess up evidence by digging it up myself."

I glanced at Charlotte, then looked back at P.D. "I also found some footprints of a man's boots. Big boots. But there was something odd about the prints. Charlotte saw them, too. It was like the boots were too big for the person wearing them. It looked like someone had stuffed socks into the toes or something. I'm not an expert at reading tracks, but I was taught by an actual Indian.

"Yeah, if it wasn't for me, the cops likely would never have traced the crime to your door, P.D.

You have my apologies. I'd heard the rifle was wiped clean of fingerprints, except for one. If you go to jail, I'll come and visit you. If they give you the gas, well, flowers on your grave will have to do."

"Wait a minute," said Charlotte, "did you say there was still one fingerprint on the gun?"

Good for Charlotte. No one else had picked up on what I'd said.

"Yes, that's right. One print, on the barrel. Or was it the receiver? It didn't match the print on the cartridges. It was not P.D.'s fingerprint. So, maybe there's a chance that he'll go free after all. As for the real killer, his best chance is to come forward and confess. Otherwise, I'd say he — or she — is doomed to die in the gas chamber."

We'd gone about as far as we could go. Ann had hardly said a word. She certainly hadn't confessed. I felt a bit dispirited. Not that I looked forward to sending her up, but the situation needed to be resolved. The dinner was over and the party was breaking up. We all rose from our chairs. The pie hadn't even been served, but we were through eating. There was a general air or disappointment in the house.

I offered to help with the dishes, but Charlotte said she and Ernie would handle the cleanup. P.D. and Rolaine had arrived together in his Jeep, so they were standing side-by-side at the door, ready to go. And that's when it happened. Rolaine opened her purse and drew forth Ann's crumpled handkerchief.

"I believe this is yours, Ann." She held it out to the other woman. "It was with Dobie's things when the undertaker returned them."

Ann not only didn't take the hanky, she backed away a couple of steps. Then she began to cry.

"I didn't — I didn't give that to your husband. It's not what you think. I gave it to — him. To Travis. He liked carrying it; he told me so. He liked taking it out of his pocket and smelling it. It must have dropped out of his pocket, at work, and Dobie picked it up. I swear. I wouldn't do such a thing to you."

She turned to P.D., and she was really turning on the tears now. "I wouldn't have let them put you in jail. I wouldn't have. I would have told. Or I would have gone to jail myself if you couldn't prove you didn't do it."

"What are you talking about?" asked P.D. "What exactly do you know?"

She sat down then, and cried for about five minutes without stopping or saying anything. Then she started talking and told us the whole tale.

"Why do I always pick the wrong men? I like to blame them, but I know it's my fault. Not all men are like the ones I choose. And Travis is worse than the others. He killed Stu. He beat up two men in town. He put a rattlesnake in Axe's car. He tried to beat me, but I ran away. And now he's gone."

"Was it Travis who sent me Stu's glass eye?"

Ann looked blank.

"That was me," said Charlotte.

"What'd you do that for?"

She shrugged. "I don't know. When I was rescuing Ernie from the cops, I found Stu's eye in the dog's water dish. I picked it up without thinking. The cops didn't see me. Later, I realized it was evidence. I didn't know what to do. I didn't want to go to the police myself; I'd have to explain. So, I mailed it to you. I figured you'd know what to do with it. I was going to write a note, explaining things, but I couldn't think of what to write. So. I just sent it."

"Thanks a lot."

"Never mind all that," said P.D. "Ann, where has this Travis fellow gone?"

"I don't know. He didn't tell me. He put in his notice at the car lot and took off."

"What?" Rolaine almost shouted. "He quit without telling me? I'm his boss! Nobody told me. I hate that man. Did he really shoot Stu? I thought you did."

"Me? No. I just covered for Travis. We were together that Sunday. We were supposed to meet in the morning. I told Mom I was going to church, but then Travis said the plans had changed and we couldn't meet until the afternoon. I was so looking forward to it. I drove over to his cabin in the mountains, early. He wasn't there. His truck wasn't there. His house was locked up."

"What's with these mistrustful, country folk?" I

complained "They're always locking their doors." But Ann ignored me.

"I checked the windows. I found one that didn't have a screen, and it was unlatched. I had an idea. I decided to surprise Travis. I got back in my truck and parked it out of sight. Then I took my things and went back to the house and climbed through the window.

"He isn't romantic like me, not usually. I have to set the mood all on my own. I'd brought along a new red nightgown. Lacy and low cut. I put it on. I found some candles and lit them in the bedroom. I found some nice music on the radio. Then I waited in the bedroom, and I didn't have to wait long. That's where I was when he came home.

"He didn't seem to notice the radio going. Maybe he thought he'd left it on himself. He was making a lot of noise in the front room. I heard him making a fire, even though it wasn't really cold. I came out of the bedroom, and his back was to me. He was trying to get the wood to light. There was something I didn't like about him. He scared me somehow.

"I said hello and he jumped a mile and turned around with his fists clenched, all angry looking. But when he saw me in my nightgown and forgot about everything else." She smiled sweetly at the memory. "He carried me to the bed and threw me on it. He's so strong. Then he took off his boots and emptied his pockets and put the stuff on the nightstand. You know, his wallet, keys, and change. There was something else. A cartridge case."

She paused and looked down at her clasped hands. "He saw me looking at it and he threw it into the little wastebasket by the bed. Then we, well, we forgot about everything for a while. I thought things would be OK. When I woke later, he was still asleep. He'd been kind of rough and had worn himself out. I dug the cartridge case out of the trash. It was a thirty-caliber carbine shell."

Ann looked up at Rolaine. "I've shot P.D.'s rifle, and that's the kind of cartridge it was. I went into the living room and the fire had gone out. I could see that he'd tried to burn something that wasn't wood. Something cloth or canvas. It was only half burned up. I jabbed at it with the poker."

She turned now to her brother. "Do you know what it was, P.D.? It was that canvas case for your rifle. I could still see the initials you'd marked on it with a pen. I didn't even know about Stu's being dead yet, but I was scared. I went back in the bedroom and dressed as quietly as I could, and I left, taking the spent cartridge and the rifle case with me. I don't know if they'll help any. Before I left, I relit the fire."

"I'm glad you're telling all of us this," said P.D. "Things will work out. Don't worry."

Ann went on with her recital.

"After I'd been home a while, he called me. I thought he might be mad or something, but he was really sweet. He said not to pay any attention to anything I'd seen at his place. He promised me he hadn't killed Stu. But how did he know Stu was dead? It wasn't in the paper until the next morning. I thought maybe he'd heard it on the radio, but I didn't really think so."

"Did you ask Travis about it?" I asked.

"Oh, no, I couldn't. He scares me. He wanted to beat me up later. The night he beat up the two guys in town, he came to my house, late at night. He had blood on his shirt. He said he was going to teach me to keep my big mouth shut, but I hadn't said anything to anyone about Travis maybe having killed Stu. He was standing on my porch. I hadn't let him in. I slammed the door shut. When he started banging against it with his shoulder, I grabbed the girls and went out the back way.

"We've been staying at Mom's since that night. I haven't told her much of anything. I just said there was a crazy man after me, an old boyfriend, and that I didn't want to involve the police.

"The next day I called Travis at work, just to feel him out, but they said he wasn't there. He told them that some kind of family emergency had come up and he'd had to leave town in a hurry. Since he didn't know when he'd be able to come back, he put in his notice. He borrowed one of the used cars, though the person I talked to said they didn't really want him to have it.

"I'm still scared of him, scared he'll come back. He warned me. But I'll tell the police everything now. I promise."

I think we were all shocked. I know I was, though I wasn't too surprised to find out an overgrown garden slug like Travis Spencer was a killer. And I was looking forward to helping send him to the gas chamber. But he'd have to be run to ground first.

Even before Ann spilled her guts to the cops, Rolaine was after me to track down Travis Spencer. I don't usually consider manhunting as part of my job, especially when the man being hunted is the size of Godzilla's baby brother. But I needed the money.

Rolaine also wanted me to keep trying to determine if Dobie's death had truly been an accident. I wasn't sure how to handle that. Maybe I could snag a copy of the autopsy somehow. Unfortunately, I didn't have any chums connected with the local coroner's office, or with the medical examiner's office in Denver. So, for now I'd concentrate on rounding up the nefarious outlaw Spencer.

I knew the cops would do their usual stuff to corral a guy on the lam, and Ann was ready to tell them everything she knew. If I wanted to beat the cops and find Travis I'd have to work fast. I needed to find a friend, or a relative, of the big used car salesman to give me some clues as to where he might go.

I talked to the folks at LeFever's Used Car Gems, but nobody seemed eager to claim him as a pal, and they couldn't name one member of his family. Rolaine was no help. Even Ann couldn't give me any information about his relatives.

That's when I thought of Jerry Clover. He might be too afraid of Travis to sell him down river, so I'd have to play my best cards to gain his cooperation.

I might even have to play the Tracy card.

20

I got on the horn and called Jeremiah's Wild Game Grubbery about seven in the morning. I hoped they wouldn't be open yet, but would be answering their phone. I needed some quiet time with Jerry. After about twenty rings he finally answered his damned phone.

"Jeremiah speaking."

"Just the man I wanted to talk to! This is Axe Hatchett, private investigator. I've got some questions for you."

"Say, aren't you the man who's dating my daughter? You better be treating her right."

"Like a spoiled princess. I like spending money on her, but my pockets aren't as deep as they used to be. I'm on a case, though. Something that might help me pick up a few bucks. I could use your help."

"That so? Would you be sending any of those bucks my direction?"

"Could be. What can you tell me about an old

hunting pal of yours, a guy named Travis Spencer?"

The line was silent for so long I was afraid he'd hung up.

"Mr. Clover?"

"That Spencer scudder is no pal of mine. I about put him in the hospital the other night. He and a couple of other thugs tried to beat me up, right in my own parking lot."

"I heard a little about that from Tracy. Looks like he skipped town, and he left behind some unpaid bills. Not only that, he's driving a stolen car. I've been hired to bring him in."

"Yeah, well, good luck with that."

"Do you happen to know if there's any place in particular where Spencer might hole up? Does he have any family? Friends in other places?"

"Look, I'm kind of busy. I've got a prosperous restaurant to run. I really don't want to talk about this Spencer mug. So, nice talking to you."

"Wait. You can give me five minutes. If not, I'll have to drive over and see you. The only reason I called you is because Tracy thought you'd be willing to help. At least, she hoped you would. It sounds like she was wrong. Seems you and her haven't gotten along all that well for a few years. To tell you the truth, she's a little disappointed in you.

"Did you know you were her hero when she was a kid? But that's all gone now. Maybe you're right, I don't need to talk to you. There's another guy I think can help me. He could use a little extra cash, and he'd love having a framed citation from the Quartz Quarry Police Department hanging on his wall. It'll probably be signed by the mayor himself. Sorry to bother you." I hung up.

I sat at my desk and whistled Red River Valley while I waited for Jerry to look me up in the phone book and call back. It only took a couple of minutes.

"Hatchett's Investigations. No nut too hard to crack. Axe speaking."

"I think we got cut off. Can't trust the damned phone company. Why would the cops give out a citation for helping to find Travis Spencer?"

"I'm not really at liberty to tell you. I can't even tell you who I'm really working for. Let me put it this way. I wouldn't be surprised if Spencer's favorite color was red. You get my meaning?"

"No."

"Come on, don't make me spell it out for you. Let's just say Spencer is probably a pretty good comrade to certain people."

"You mean like the commies?"

"Enough said, Jerry."

"So, if I help you out I could get this nice framed citation, something I could hang up in the restaurant, and some cash besides? And Tracy might think of me as her hero again?"

"Yeah, but don't be a sap. It's not worth it; I don't know why I called you. Spencer is a pretty dangerous character."

"There's not many folks I'm afraid of, Mr. Hatchett."

"Call me Axe."

"Listen, I used to go hunting with Travis. He's got a place up in the hills, way out in the sticks."

"You mean besides his mountain home outside of town here?"

"Oh, yeah. Real remote, that's what I'd call it. I went up there a couple of times with him, years ago. There's a lake up there and the fishing's great. Nice little cabin. Hell, I don't even know if it's really his. There's three old cabins up there. Two of them are falling apart. The third one Travis fixed up himself.

"He hauled a couple of rolls of tarpaper up there and patched the roof. He re-chinked the log walls, and got the fireplace chimney fixed and cleared out. He stomped around and chased off the pack rats, then he built a new door and put a padlock on it. He made shutters for the window and put a lock on them. Nobody stopped him, so I guess nobody really owns the place."

"Sounds like a great hideout. You willing to draw a map for me?"

"I can't."

"Yeah. Tracy was hoping you'd help, but — "

"No, it's not that. I want to help. A map wouldn't do you any good. You'd never be able to find the place. You ever been over to Cinnamon Wells?"

"Sure. It's about eighty miles from here. Not

much over there but some starving cattle ranches, and Porcupine Peak."

"Right. Real remote. To get to Travis's cabin you've got to drive through Cinnamon Wells and turn off on this old dirt road. Used to be a stage-coach road. You can get a car down it, but it's got a lot of washboard, and a lot of rocks. Then, about five or six miles along, you come to a road that's even worse. You'd have to have a Jeep to get up it, or walk. Travis used to keep a beat-up Army Jeep up there, parked in an old barn. He'd drive up there in his car, start up the Jeep with jumper ca-bles, and go on up to the lake. The cabins are off in the trees a ways, out of sight of the water. You couldn't find the place with a map, I swear."

"So, what are you suggesting?"

"I'd have to go with you. Take a day off."

I didn't relish the idea of being trapped in a car with the mouthy and prevaricating Jerry Clover for a total of a hundred-and-sixty miles or more round trip.

"Are you sure you couldn't draw a really good, detailed, map for me?"

"I'm sure. Like I said, I was only up there a couple of times. It might be hard for even me to find. But I can do it. Old Eagle-Eye Clover can find the spot. But I got to be there in person, so to speak."

"OK. I'll have to get back to you. There's a cou-ple of details I'll have to arrange. Let me call you back later."

"Sure. I'll be here. You can count on me."

I hung up, then dialed Bram Duckers at Happy Trails Shooting Range. He was there.

"Bram? This is Axe"

"Hey. You got something for me?"

"Maybe. How'd you like to take a trip over to Cinnamon Wells and beyond?"

"I'd have to take time off. I don't know. I already missed a day when I got beat up. I don't think they'd be too happy my talking time off right now."

"Happy Trails not happy? Listen, it's important. You don't have to take more than one day off. You'll be helping me track down Travis Spencer. He might have killed Stu Slaughter."

"Wow. So, I was right!"

"It happens now and then. Listen, I need a good man with me. I don't want to tackle Spencer on my own. What do you say?"

"Well, Happy Trails won't be happy."

"You already said that. Let them cry a little. Come on. You can bring your bow and arrows."

"It's not just the shooting range I'm thinking of, it's Celeste. She doesn't want me working for you anymore. It was her idea to keep the police out of my getting beat up."

"Women. You can't figure them out. Listen, right now you're her little woodly squidlums. But wait and see what happens once the kid is born. You'll be out the window. She'll have eyes only for the baby, and she'll want a big strong capable husband to watch after her and the tyke. Trust me.

"It won't be long before she'll be giving you grief for not standing up to Spencer. It won't matter that it's not fair. And it won't matter that it was her idea. She'll treat you like you're a coward. Come on, Bram, you've got more backbone than that. Happy Trails won't fire you, not for missing one more day. They like you. And I'll pay you better than they do; you know that. What do you say?"

"You certain Spencer's a killer?"

"Practically positive."

"Cops will leave us alone?"

"They won't know a thing. They've still got their heads stuck in the mud."

"Think it'll come to shooting?"

"Let's hope not. It could."

"Wouldn't mind getting a crack at that big boy. He owes me."

"Sure he does. And what better revenge than to put him in the jug. This is big for you, Bram. I've never involved you in something like this. I need your cool head, and your gun hand."

"Murder ain't no joke."

"Sure ain't."

"Can I talk to Celeste first?"

"No. She'd only talk you out of it. You don't wear diapers."

He was silent a moment.

"Sure. I'm in. When do we go?"

"That's my boy. Soon. Maybe tomorrow. We've

got another guy going with us. I don't like it, but he's the only guy who can take us to where Spencer might be holed up. It's Jerry Clover, the other guy Spencer beat up the night you got attacked. I've got to call him back. Listen, can we take your car? I'm not eager to take mine over rough country roads."

"Celeste will need the car."

"OK. I'll find out what Jerry drives. I know he's got a truck or van big enough to haul a dead buffalo. But that might be too big a vehicle. I'll see what else he's got. And I'll have to call my client, see if it's all right for me to hire two helpers. I'll call you back. OK?"

"Sure. I'm in. We'll fix that Spencer's wagon."

I hung up and called Jerry back. Lilly answered.

"Mrs. Clover?"

"That's me, honey. What can I do for you?"

"This is Axe Hatchet, your daughter's love-struck boyfriend."

"Why, howdy. I've heard all about you. I wish you had a more regular job."

"Me too. Maybe someday. Is your husband available?"

"Yes. He told me something about going on a manhunt. I hope that's not true."

"Not a manhunt exactly. We're just going over to Cinnamon Wells to look up a fisherman friend of Jerry's."

"Travis Spencer ain't a friend of Jerry's."

"Everything will be fine. Don't worry. There'll

be three of us. We'll be careful."

"Well, I can't never tell Jerry what to do any-how. I'll get him for you."

I held the line while she fetched Pop Clover. In a moment, he got on the phone.

"Jerry? You up for tomorrow?"

"So soon?"

"The sooner the better."

"I guess that'll be all right"

"What kind of car do you drive?"

"Olds. Woody."

"Mind taking it to Cinnamon Wells? My boat's not made for that kind of terrain. It's kind of a sis-sy car."

"The Olds ain't a sissy. It'll go anywhere. Why, I've had it to the top of most of the mountains in Colorado."

"I'm sure you have. The gas is on me. Can you pick me up about seven in the morning?"

"I'll be there. And I'll be heeled."

"Not necessary. I'll be bringing along a young tough who spits in the eye of danger and sneers at trouble. He'll be armed. So will I. See you in the morning."

"You don't think Spencer will try nothing fun-ny, do you?"

"Naw. He doesn't have much of a sense of hu-mor. All we want to do is find him. Then we'll turn matters over to the cops in Cinnamon Wells. Boy will they be happy."

"All right. If you think we'll be safe."

"Safe as a church social, with guns."

I said goodbye, hung up the phone, and then called Bram back.

"Tomorrow," I told him. "We'll pick you up a little after seven in the morning."

"Sweet. I'll be ready, and I'll be packing."

"A suitcase? It's only going to take a day."

"A gun. A gat. I'll be packing iron."

"Got you. See you in the morning."

I put in a call to Rolaine and told her about the extra expenses. She was fine with that and wished me luck. Now I had the hard call to make. Tracy. I thought maybe I should drop by Rocko's and tell her in person, but I was afraid she'd whack me with a frying pan. Instead, I dialed the diner. A mean voice answered.

"Tracy?"

"Is that you, my little Marmalade and Mackerel Sandwich?"

"None other. Listen, something's come up. I'm going on a kind of a manhunt. We're going to try to smoke Travis Spencer out of his den."

"The guy you think killed Slaughter?"

"The same."

"You said 'we'."

"I'm taking Bram Duckers with me. I've told you about him. And — someone else. Your Pop."

"You're taking Pop on a manhunt?"

"I have to. I need him to show me where Spencer might be holed up. Over by Cinnamon Wells."

"Listen, this could be dangerous. For you.

Whatever you do, don't let him drive. I've ridden with Pop in the car. You haven't. He whistles and sings cowboy songs, both off key. He spits tobacco out the window, and sometimes it doesn't go out the window at all. He stops at every little burg he comes to and buys a burger. He talks to gas station attendants for like an hour. You might not survive."

"I'll watch my back. So, you're OK with all this?"

"You need the money, and nothing will happen to Pop. He just got beat up; his luck has to change."

"All right. We're leaving tomorrow morning. I'll call you when we get back."

"Swell. Oh, and Axe?"

"Yes?"

"Promise me. Please."

"What?"

"Don't get car sick."

"I promise. I'll eat a light breakfast. Not at Rocko's."

I said goodbye to Tracy, my little Moldy Crumpet. It occurred to me I hadn't told Jerry where to pick me up, and so I called him back and gave him directions to my house. I was set. I was ready. I was scared.

21

Pop Clover was right on time the next morning. In fact, he was honking his horn before I could get out the door He didn't comment on my having been named Snake Bane Craven the last time we'd met, so I let it go.

His car was a mess. It had no-doubt started out as a nice enough Oldsmobile station wagon. A woody. But it looked like Jerry had spent the last couple of years of ownership trying to make the car smaller. The front end was crunched. The rear end was an accordion. Two of the doors were collapsed. Even the hood and the top had big dents in them, like he'd rolled the thing a couple of times.

Fortunately, the inside was as big as ever. I got into the front passenger's seat, vowing to switch to the back seat when we picked up Bram. I was taking Tracy at her word. I was wearing my cloth raincoat, my hat was pulled low, and I had a pocket full of cotton balls to use as earplugs. I was prepared for errant tobacco-juice spitting and off-key cowboy songs.

I guided Pops to Bram's duplex and we picked him up there. Bram was waiting on the front stoop. Even from that distance I could see that Celeste had exaggerated his injuries. His nose was the same bulbous nub it'd always been. The front door was open and Celeste stood in it, glaring through the screen door, wearing a frumpy bathrobe, her arms crossed over her big belly. Bram turned back to her, offered a weak wave, and ambled down the sidewalk to join us. I got out of the front seat and relocated in the back.

When Bram slid in beside Jerry, I said: "You're wearing that damned cowboy hat. Too bad it's not full of sandwiches. Take it off, will you? We're on a job."

He reluctantly complied. I sailed the hat into the back of the station wagon. Jerry took a look at Duckers. He apparently didn't recognize Bram as the guy he'd gone poaching with. Good old invisible Bram. I made introductions.

"I remember you," said Jerry. "It was you and me and Travis that day when we were hunting and those two guys with the rifles came up on us and made us give up our elk. Mighty fine twelve-point bull, too."

"It was one guy," said Bram. "and he was only carrying a revolver, and the elk didn't have anywhere near twelve-points."

"Guess you don't remember right."

"I remember all right. And now we're headed over to roundup Spencer for killing that same guy. Small world, huh?"

Jerry slammed on the brakes and a car behind us had to do the same. Jerry's face was pasty white.

"We don't know for sure Travis is the killer," I said, trying to soften things. "But everything will be duck soup. Don't worry. Come on, let's get going."

"You didn't tell me what I was getting into," Jerry complained to me, hitting the gas pedal again.

"That's because I knew you were a guy that's never felt a moment of fear in his entire life. That's what Tracy says."

That shut him up.

Everything Tracy had told me about her Pop's road manners turned out to be true. He sang, he whistled, he spat. We hadn't gone twenty miles before he spotted a town that consisted of two buildings and a sign and wanted to stop for a burger. I told him to forget it; it was nowhere near lunchtime. Then he started worrying about his gas tank, thinking maybe it wasn't full enough. But he'd already told me earlier that he'd filled it up that morning before picking me up.

The one thing Tracy hadn't warned me about was Pop's driving. When he wasn't tailgating he was getting in front of cars and slowing way down until they honked. He honked his own horn plenty, too, mostly for no reason. He took the curves too fast, straddled the white line whenever possible, and nearly went off the road a couple of times when he was rubbernecking cows by the side of the road. It wasn't long before both Bram and I were volunteering to drive, but Jerry wouldn't hear of it.

"Sorry," he explained, "I don't let anyone drive the Olds. They might not know how to handle it."

The road was a nice enough blacktop for about forty miles. Then we crossed into a less prosperous county and hit a long stretch of pavement that'd been patched and re-patched until it looked like a hobo's socks. Then the black top petered out entirely and gave way to gravel.

About halfway to Cinnamon Wells we stopped at a little town called Claybank Corners for lunch. Jerry'd been hollering he couldn't go any longer without chow. We ate hot roast beef sandwiches, with damn little beef, extra gravy, and bread that was at least a day old. We bought gas there, too. Fortunately, the attendant proved surly, so Jerry gave up talking to him after only half-an-hour.

What with the bad driving and the bad roads, the too long lunch, and the chat with the petrol pumper, it was around eleven by the time we hit Cinnamon Wells. Jerry was ready to stop for a little snack. I told him he could eat when we'd established that Travis was in his little cozy cabin.

"Don't forget what we came here for, Jerry," I told hm. "Got it?"

"Yeah, yeah. I got it, and I've got something for you, amigo. What's Spanish for a horse's patootie?"

"I believe that's hossy-end-a. Why?"

"Think on it."

We drove through town, then took a bad dirt road until it turned off into a worse road. This must have been the old stage trail Jerry had mentioned. At some point it'd been widened a bit, maybe leveled some, but there was plenty of washboard. And rocks from the cliffs on each side had tumbled onto the roadway and hadn't been removed. We stayed on this route for about twenty minutes, passing by stands of pine and aspen. We finally reached a spot of forest that Jerry recognized, and he pulled off onto the sandy shoulder.

"Here's the place," Jerry almost whispered. He was turning white around the gills. "I'll show you where that old barn is."

We piled out of the Olds, shook the kinks out of our bones, and walked into the trees. There was a wide spot that might allow the passage of a car, and it was covered with pine needles. Pops led us about fifty yards to a little meadow in the middle of which was an old board shack that might once have been a small barn. It was weathered gray and there were holes in its shake roof.

A big double door had had its hinges replaced at some point, though they were already rusty. There was a hasp with a padlock. It was a combination lock; my lock-picking skills didn't extend to that kind of padlock. I looked at Bram and raised my eyebrows. Without a word he calmly hauled out a big forty-five from somewhere in his clothes and shot off the hinged end of the hasp. Jerry didn't jump more than enough to clear a two-story building.

"I was thinking of something a little less noisy, Bram, like prying the hasp off with a tire iron. I hope you-know-who didn't hear that shot."

Bram turned red. "Sorry. I tend to think in terms of guns."

We swung the big doors open. Inside was the smell of dust and there was something covered with a sheet of water-stained canvas. We pulled the cloth aside, revealing a car.

"'50 Chevy Bel Air. Two door. Brown" I said. It was the same damned car they'd been teasing me with for over a week. "That's the car Travis borrowed from the car lot. But the license plate is the wrong number. He must have switched plates at some point. Chances are the car owner hasn't even noticed. Folks don't pay much attention to their plates once they're on the car."

"The Jeep ain't here," Jerry pointed out.

"Well, I guess we know where Travis Spencer is. Fishing on his little lake," I said.

"Now what?" asked Bram.

I looked at Pops. He was sweating. His face was about the same white as aspen bark.

"Well," I said, "one of us will have to drive

back to Cinnamon Wells and find the police station. It'll take a cool head. Jerry, are you up to it?"

He gave me a relieved look.

"I can do it. I'll drive fast."

"Don't. Slow and steady wins the race. Tell the
cops we've got a murder suspect cornered. A big
guy. Bring back as many coppers as you can. I'm
not sure how large the Cinnamon Wells Police
Department is, so you might have to bring everybody, including the meter maid. Get going."

Jerry didn't have to be asked twice. He backed
away from the barn, turned around and fairly
high-tailed it for his car. When he was gone, Bram
lit up a corncob pipe he favors and I set fire to a
cheap cigar.

"We going to have to go up and get him?"
Bram asked.

I shrugged. "I don't know how else we're going
to get him. It'll be a hike. At least he won't be expecting us."

I was wrong about that. We'd been standing
around smoking for close to forty-five minutes,
wondering if the troops were about to show up,
when we heard a noise up in the woods. The narrow Jeep trail that doubtless led up to the lake was
only a few yards from the barn. In a couple of
minutes a man looking about the size of a boxcar
came around a curve of the trail.

It was Spencer. He was carrying a big bow and
had a quiver of arrows over one shoulder. No
doubt he'd been out hunting for food and had

heard Bram's pistol when he'd shot off the lock on the barn. When he saw us, he roared like a lion, skidded to a stop, raised the bow, and fitted an arrow to the string.

I reached under my raincoat and fumbled out my Browning High Power. Bram was quicker and had his forty-five in his hand almost instantly.

We were both too slow. Travis let fly the arrow and I felt it whizz about a foot from my right ear. I snapped off a couple of quick shots but I knew they'd both missed.

Travis was still about twenty yards away. He was fitting another arrow to his bowstring. I wondered what Bram was doing. I shouldn't have wondered. He was taking a careful two-handed aim at Travis. His gun let out a bang and Travis dropped his bow, clutching at his bleeding left wrist. Then he grabbed a hunting knife from his belt and charged us, bellowing like a cheapskate gorilla that's just been short-changed.

I don't know what went wrong with Bram and me. We both froze. I think it was that God-awful sound coming out of Travis that did the trick. We just stood there while the huge maniac came at us with his knife.

He went straight for Bram, slashing a savage arc with the knife. He connected with Bram's face and my partner went to the ground.

I got my pistol back up, the grip slippery with sweat. Travis sprang at me and tried to stick me with his big Arkansas toothpick. He barely missed, cutting away part of my coat sleeve, then kicked me in the stomach.

I went down, clutching my gut. He kicked me again, this time on the side of the head. My hat flew off and pretty little stars circled my cranium.

I looked up in time to see Travis bring back his leg for another kick, but Bram's gun banged again, and the bullet came out the front of Travis's knee. Some bits of bone hit my face and stuck. I pointed my High Power at the man, but I didn't pull the trigger. He was down on the ground, rolling, screaming, and clutching his bloody leg.

I hurried over to check on my partner. He was mopping off his face with a bandanna. The knife had sliced open his forehead. I hoped it wouldn't scar when it healed.

Several more minutes passed before Jerry and his following of cops showed up. In the meantime, I bound up Bram's wound with his bandanna. He really did look like an Indian now. We tore about half of Travis's pant leg off and tied it around his leg. There was a lot of blood, and a lot of noise. I hoped he wouldn't die before we could get him to a hospital.

As it turned out, Cinnamon Wells had three cop cars, and two of them had followed Jerry's Olds out to where we were waiting. One of the cops, wearing a huge cowboy hat like Bram's, knew a thing or two about medicine and was able to stop most of Travis's bleeding. We folded down the back seat of Jerry's station wagon and hoisted the murder suspect into the back.

"Look at all that blood," said Jerry, looking a bit green. "How am I going to get that out? Guy's going to spoil my car."

We caravanned back to town, me driving the borrowed Chevy with Bram in the passenger's seat, and cruised to Cinnamon Wells' pretty two-storied brick hospital. They sewed up Travis, and squirted some fresh blood into him, and it looked like he might live. His knee was probably ruined, but he wouldn't be needing it much longer.

They sewed up Bram's knife cut, and cleaned and bandaged the scuff on my head and picked the pieces of Spencer's knee out of my cheek, then Bram and Jerry and I tramped out of the place surrounded by happy cowboy cops. Oh, boy! A real live murder suspect, right here in Cinnamon Wells! It was like Christmas for these guys.

They took us down to the police station, a one-story blond brick affair, where we filed into a room where a small evaporative cooler wheezed in one window. We sat in wooden chairs at wooden tables and gave our versions of what had happened and why.

I was feeling queasy. I wasn't sure if Travis was a wanted man yet. I was pretty sure Ann had talked to the cops by now, but I wasn't certain. I might be in some thick soup if Travis wasn't even wanted yet. But I was in luck. The Cinnamon Wells cops already knew that the Quartz Quarry cops were after Travis Spencer. For murder.

After a while, the cops decided they'd had as much fun as they could get out of us and they let us go. We headed home.

Jerry manned his beloved Olds. Bram and I motored back to Quartz Quarry in the Chevy. It did indeed run like a top. The gears shifted like greased butter, and the motor purred like a kitten full of milk. It had a lot of miles on it, the odometer said seventy-thousand, but whoever had owned it had loved it. It had scarcely a distinguishing mark on it.

If the former proud owner had neglected one thing, it was the paint. It had not been waxed for some time, and a dull film had formed on the brown finish. It was nearly perfect for a detective's car.

I made up my mind right then and there to do what I could to take Tracy's three-hundred dollars in tip money and turn it over for this little mud-brown beauty. That way, if I needed a car for tailing somebody, I could just switch to the Chevy, and Tracy could drive the Ruby Roadrunner instead.

When we got back to town I called Tracy. I told her about our capturing Spencer.

"And boy do I have a surprise in store for you," I told her.

"You didn't get car sick?"

"No. I was only kicked in the head and the stomach. But I kept my breakfast and my lunch down. I found something for you to buy with your tip money. Runs like grandpa's old pocket watch."

"Swell. Tell me it's red."

"It's brown, but you can have the red one if I can get it. Listen, I'm coming by Rocko's as soon as I can. Tell Cookie to burn a couple of egg sandwiches for me, will you?"

22

With Travis Spencer safely put away in jail, awaiting a murder conviction, all I had to do to please my client, Rolaine, was to determine if her husband had died accidently, or had been murdered. I hadn't been able to get hold of a copy of Dobie's autopsy report. My next step was to track down the mysterious biology major who had tipped off the widow about the autopsy results.

However, I was spared the trouble of having to do this, and all because someone gave Blythe Bliss a little present.

I came home from the office one evening — Bram and I were working on a new case involving mysteriously-disappearing chickens — and found officer Bliss sitting in her lawn chair, wearing civvies, sipping a beer, and smiling like her bank account couldn't be bigger.

"Howdy, neighbor."

"Howdy yourself, Blythe. What's with the big smile?"

"Someone's sweet on me."

"I would think the whole police department would be sweet on you. Someone special?"

"Don't know. It's a secret admirer. And he sent me a present. I found it in my 'In' box this morning."

"Pearls? A mink? Chewing tobacco?"

"Better than any of them. I'll show you." She wriggled around in her chair and brought up a thick cylinder that looked like some kind of rolled-up parchment scroll. Then she stood up and unrolled the damned thing, holding it by one hand above her head. Biggest snakeskin I ever saw.

"Ain't it pretty?"

"It's a beaut all right. I see it has rattles. What is it, a diamondback?"

She nodded, and smiled like it was a big diamond ring. At least it had diamonds.

"I don't know how they cured it. Rock salt, maybe. That's how Daddy used to do it. Do you recognize it?"

"Am I supposed to? Wait, is that from the snake that killed LeFever?"

"I don't see how it can be any other. I wonder how my secret sweetie got ahold of it."

"Who knows? From the coroner, maybe. Is it something you particularly wanted?"

"Folks down at the station know I've had a hankering for a great big rattlesnake skin since I was knee high to a grasshopper. And now I've got one. Daddy never shot one this big."

I had a thought. It was a good one.

"Say, could I borrow that thing?"

"Borrow it? You can't even touch it. I'm going to nail it to my bedroom wall so it's the first thing I see when I wake up in the morning."

"That's fine, but you don't need to do that this minute. Let me borrow it, just for an hour or so."

"No! I wouldn't even let you take a picture of it."

"Listen, if I show that skin to the right guy, he might be able to tell me if Dobie LeFever was murdered or died accidently."

I could see some hesitation in her predatory doe eyes.

"That sounds like a police matter. But since the possible murderer is dead himself, it might be — what do the courts call it? — a moot point."

"If it becomes police business, they'll confiscate that hide and you'll never see it again. I won't do that. Come on, neighbor! I'll guard it with my life."

"You better. Know what happens to you if anything happens to that skin?"

"A slow death, with lots of suffering along the way."

"You got it. It's not just the skin I like, it's got sentimental value."

"I hope your secret admirer reveals himself soon."

"Me too. I just hope he ain't short."

She lovingly rolled the hide back up and reluctantly handed it to me.

"Have it back in an hour or I'll send a patrol car after you."

"I'll do my best."

I got into the Nash, stuck the rolled hide in the glove compartment, and headed over to Dr. Eben Mulford's house. I figured he'd be home. He seldom went out. I climbed the steep steps to his front door with the snakeskin under my arm, and gave the secret knock-ring-knock signal that would allow me admittance. In a couple of minutes Mulford opened the door.

"Axe, old fellow, back so soon? I'm honored."

"As you should be."

Mulford was quietly smacking his lips.

"Come in, come in."

I came in.

"Have I interrupted another one of your meals?" I asked.

"Well, yes. I've just been munching a repast of baby clams on banana bread. Open faced, of course."

"Of course. Let's head back to your kitchen. I'll let you get back to your meal."

He led the way through the living room and down the hall leading to his bright kitchen. I kept my eye out for stray snakes the whole time.

"Coffee?" he asked.

"No, I don't want to trouble you. I've just got a couple of quick questions for you. About snakes."

He sighed, and took his place at the breakfast-nook table. I sat across from him, trying not to look at his nasty little sandwich, and showed him the rolled-up rattler hide.

"Brought you a little treat." I said.

"Not on the table, please. You'll take away my appetite. Perhaps you can unroll it on the linoleum, if you must."

"Huh? I thought you'd be pleased."

"If it was intact and alive I would be very pleased. But in its present state — I feel like I'm attending a funeral. Not your fault. Let's see it. Quite long, isn't it?"

I was unrolling it on the floor.

"Close to eight feet, with the head gone, if the newspapers got it right. This is the snake that killed Dobie LeFever."

"Excuse me. Those are the mortal remains of the unfortunate viper that defended itself by biting LeFever."

"Well, sure. Have it your way. What can you tell me about this rattler by looking at its hide? Anything?"

"It appears to be the outer covering of a very fine example of the Eastern Diamondback rattlesnake."

"That's it? Nothing unusual about it?"

He nibbled at his clams and banana bread and gave me an impish smile.

"Do my observations disappoint you?"

"In a way. We'd talked about hybrids the last time I was here. Could this fellow be a hybrid?"

"What's your own thought?"

"I don't have any. One rattler looks the same as another in my world."

"Your ignorance appalls me."

He finished one sandwich, spread peanut butter on a second slice of bread, and covered it with slimy dime-sized clams from a tin.

"Come on, Eben. Don't play with me."

"Play with you? Why, I'm only trying to help in your education. Do you see the brown and the black diamond patterns on the — remains?"

"Of course I do."

"Those markings give the snake its name. Diamondback."

"Thanks. And I guess the Bronx accent is the reason it's called an Eastern Diamondback."

"I hadn't thought of that. Perhaps. However, do you see the white-and-black raccoon stripes on the tail, near the rattles?"

"Of course."

"Eastern Diamondbacks don't have those markings."

"Eureka! Anything else?"

"Well, what about the greenish tinge?"

"I noticed that. Maybe it's not ripe yet."

"The Mojave rattler, among others, often has a greenish coloring. It also has stripes on the end of its tail."

"Are you telling me what I hope you're telling me? I remember you said that the Mojave has a lot of neurotoxin in its venom. If this snake was a cross between a Mojave and an Eastern Diamond-back, then that might explain Dobie Le Fever's dubious autopsy findings."

"Indeed. LeFever may not have been murdered after all."

"I'm happy to hear that, believe me. So, how did this fellow get so big? Are Mojave rattlers big guys too?"

"The Mojave usually achieves a length of no more than four feet. This 'fellow,' as you call him, likely became so big because he was raised in captivity, and was fed well and often. Doubtless the parents were also captive serpents, hence their opportunity to mate. I think your little mystery might be solved.

"Now, please, remove that sad reminder of reptilian mortality from my sight."

I rolled up the hide and tried to stuff it in my inside jacket pocket. It didn't fit. It looked like I was trying to hide a flag pole. Eben and I talked for a few more minutes about snakes, the Wife of Bath, fine cuisine, and sundry other topics. Then I glanced at my watch and winced.

"I'd like to stay longer, Eben, but I've got to return this skin to its proud owner before she puts out an all-points bulletin on me. Enjoy the rest of your meal," I said. "And, thanks. You've been a big help. I'll let myself out."

"Good seeing you again. Oh, and Axe, I've let Chauncey out for a little stroll. If you meet up with him while you're making your egress, tip your hat and smile for him. He appreciates such attentions."

I made my way through the back hall and living room as carefully as I could. Chauncey? Who-and-what-the-hell was Chauncey? A Russell's viper? An anaconda? I wished I was wearing waders. As I left the house and jigged down the front steps, an unbiased observer might have wondered if I was late for my own funeral.

I drove over to my office and looked at my mail. It was disappointing, as usual. I decided to call the widow LeFever. She answered on the third ring, a little breathlessly.

"It's me, Axe," I said. "You got a minute?"

"Of course."

"Good. I've got a couple of things to tell you. First of all, let me assure you that your husband wasn't murdered. It was an accident. Dobie was bitten by some kind of hybrid rattlesnake — two snakes in one you might say. I got ahold of its hide and showed it to my snake expert friend."

"Then Stu didn't murder Dobie?"

"No."

"I'm relieved to hear that. Maybe it shouldn't matter to me, but it does. Thanks for finding out what really happened. What else do you have to tell me?"

"I think I know who pushed Dobie into the lake."

"Oh?" She sounded wary.

"Don't worry, I'm not going to tell the cops. But

you might tell your boyfriend to watch his temper. I figure P.D. pushed your husband into the lake because he didn't like the way Dobie treated you. I doubt if he was really trying to drown him. Maybe he was just passing by the lake and saw Dobie out on the pier and decided to put a scare into him. What do you say to that?"

She was silent for a moment. "Well, maybe you've figured it out. P.D. is my lover. He hasn't admitted to pushing Dobie into the water, but I think you might be right. P.D.'s not always sensible."

"That's OK. Not many of us are."

23

I finally got my Hornet back from that louse, Otto. He actually tried to charge me. It ran fine, but somehow it wasn't the same. Its spirit was broken.

Thanks to Rolaine, I was able to trade it straight across for the Ruby Roadrunner. Not only that, but the grateful widow let Tracy buy the old brown Chevy for only two-hundred-and-fifty bucks. Sweet deal!

I tried giving Tracy the Nash, but she wanted the Chevy.

"I couldn't park the Ruby Roadrunner behind Rocko's. Somebody'd swipe it."

"Do you mean side-swipe it, or steal it?"

"Both. You keep the Nash and I'll learn to drive the Chevy."

"That red yacht is a lousy detective's car."

"You can borrow my car when you're on a case. Say it's a deal."

"OK. It's a deal."

Tracy hadn't driven for a long time, so I gave her a few lessons. We hardly fought at all while I put her and her car through their paces, but I had to keep my mouth shut a lot.

Not long after I'd taken all the loose ends of the LeFever case and tied them into a granny knot, the carnival came to town. Only, it wasn't our town. It had set up in Wavering Haze, about forty miles from Quartz Quarry. I assured Tracy that in a couple of weeks or so they'd dismantle the whole shebang and move it over to our fair city, but she wasn't taking any chances.

"What if some kid falls off the Ferris wheel and dies?" she asked me. "They might close down the whole carnival, the saps, and I'd miss it. What then?"

"Then you can be glad you weren't the one that was killed. Look at it that way."

But it was no dice. So we planned a trip to drive over to Wavering Haze and avail ourselves of the fun. Tracy decided she didn't want to drive the Chevy that far; she was awfully maternal about her new ride. We took the Nash, and I had her drive. A little experience on the open road would do her good.

We arrived at the fair-grounds where the carnival was being held right around dusk. It was all lit up like somebody's very merry Christmas. There was a Ferris wheel, a merry-go-round, and some honest-to-God real horses walking around in a circle with a bunch of scared and squealing little kids on their backs. There was a tiny train that ran through the carnival grounds, and there were games, and carnies hawking food everywhere. Tracy went for the food first.

"I've got to build up my strength for the games," she told me.

While I watched in horror, she downed a foot-long chilidog, a bag of peanuts, a big cloud of blue cotton candy, and washed it all down with something that purported to be elderberry fizz. I settled for a normal-sized plain hotdog and some lemonade and I still got heartburn. When Tracy had fortified herself sufficiently, she headed straight for the baseball pitch.

The object was to throw baseballs, made lumpy by too many bad pitches, at some wooden pins, with their bottoms weighted with lead, shaped like milk bottles. The tops of these particular pins were carved into the shapes of various animal heads. Some of them had had their noses or ears knocked off.

Tracy was a champ. She toppled over enough pins to win one of the ugliest stuffed animals I've ever seen. I think it was supposed to be a bunny, but it looked more like a long-eared monkey with its face punched in. And it was orange.

"Isn't it beautiful?" Tracy asked, proudly. "It looks exactly like my idea of the Easter Bunny."

"I'd hate to see your idea of Santa Claus."

"You're just jealous. OK, it's your turn. Pick a game."

"Don't you want to throw some more base-balls?"

"Naw. It's too easy. Pick something else."

I looked around. Not far from us was a Big Striker game. You know the one. There's this pole, about twenty-feet tall, painted up like a thermometer. You take this mallet about the size of something Goliath would use for a gavel, and you swing it down on this hinged plate. There's a metal dingus that slides on a cable that goes all the way to the top of the pole. And there's a bell at the top that rings when some lucky rube hits the plate just right.

It's rigged. Some lumberjack comes along and gives it his best, to show off to his girl, and the metal dingus only goes up about halfway. The carny running the game can do it so the bell rings every time. He's happy to show you. Generally the carny's a bruiser, but if you watch him carefully when he's swinging the mallet you'll see he's not really putting all his muscle into it. Then watch when some little guy steps forward to try his luck. The dingus goes way higher than when the lumberjack hit it. In other words, you've got to hit it just right.

I handed over my two tickets, spit on my hands, and swung the mallet about half as hard as I could. The dingus went about halfway. I turned over more tickets, and this time I swung the mallet harder. Too hard. I didn't come close to ringing the bell. I tried it one more time; I was getting the feel of the thing. Tracy let out a big squeal because this time I struck the plate with almost exactly the right amount of force. The dingus stopped no more than a foot from the bell.

"That's it," I said to Tracy. "I'm not wasting any more tickets."

"He should get something for that," Tracy said to the carny. "Give him a consolation prize. How about that pair of fuzzy pink dice?"

"You kiddin'? Guy's got to ring the bell. No prizes if he don't."

"That's not fair. He was so close."

"Life ain't fair, lady."

"OK, then how about we trade prizes? I'll give you my beautiful bunny for those fuzzy dice."

"Cause your husband didn't hit the bell? Cause he did perzactly nothin'? No deal. I'd get in Dutch with the boss."

"Come on, buddy," I said, "trade with her. It's worth it just to keep her out of your hair. Trust me."

The guy took a good look at Tracy's stubborn face.

"OK, OK. But don't come back." He handed over the fuzzy dice and Tracy gave up the rabbit thing. Boy was I relieved; I wouldn't have to look at it anymore.

"Here," Tracy handed me the dice. "You can hang them on the rearview mirror of the Ruby Roadrunner. You're my hero."

"Thanks. Now what? We could ride the Ferris

wheel."

I only said this because I'd gotten the impression that Tracy was scared of the thing. I hadn't been able to scare her with Stu Slaughter's glass eye, and she was bored to tears by the live rattlesnake Travis Spencer had put in my car. Maybe just threatening her with the Ferris wheel would shake her up. But I hadn't thought things through very clearly. She took me up on my offer.

"Sure, let's ride the Ferris wheel. Look how pretty it is with all its lights. I hope it stops when we're right on top, then we can swing back and forth, and look at all the tiny people down on the ground."

That about turned my stomach. I hate Ferris wheels. In fact, I don't care for heights at all.

"No," I said. "It's just a kids' ride. Let's ride something grown up, like that little train."

"They should have boats, and a tunnel of love."

"How could they have boats? They'd have to dig a canal every time they switched towns."

"I suppose. I guess the Ferris wheel will have to do."

"Look! See those real-live horses over there? Let's ride on those, pretend we're cowboys."

"No. I want the Ferris wheel."

I wasn't about to admit to her that I was scared of the fool things. Maybe it wouldn't be as bad as I remembered. We got in line, and when our turn came I handed over more tickets and we climbed into one of the death cars. The carny in charge of the ride fastened the safety bar for us, but it felt loose to me. The wheel started up, and in a sickeningly short time we were rising up into the air. And damned if the carny didn't stop the thing when Tracy and I were right at the very top.

"Isn't it gorgeous!" Tracy said. "Look at all the lights. And the stars are coming out. Look how small everything looks from up here. Can you see our car in the parking lot?"

I couldn't see anything. I had my eyes tight shut, and both my arms were wrapped around the metal stanchion on my side of the seat.

"What's the matter?" Tracy asked. "Don't tell me you're scared of a little old Ferris wheel? It's a kids' ride."

"I'm not a kid. I'm OK, just a little queasy. Probably the hotdog I ate."

"No, I think you're scared. Say, if I rock the seat back and forth will it make you even more afraid?"

"Don't do it. Please. If you swing the seat back and forth I'll slide under the safety bar and fall to my death."

"No you won't. You're fine. So, if I rock the seat really hard and fast, will you ask me to marry you?"

"No, I won't even invite you to my funeral. Come on, Tracy, let up. It's not funny."

"Sure, I'll let up as soon as you propose to me."

"Never. I'd sooner marry that stuffed monkey you traded away."

"It was a bunny. You'd rather marry a stuffed bunny than me? Fine, have it your way."

We finally started moving again. In about a year we reached the ground and I shakily clambered out of the iron monster. I suspected Tracy was pretty mad. She didn't speak for a while, and we just wandered around aimlessly. Finally, she spoke.

"Axe, I'm sorry. That was mean of me. You were scared and I made things worse for you. I don't blame you for not wanting to marry me. I must take after my Pop. A mean streak a mile wide."

"You don't take after your Pop. Nothing could be further from the truth. You must take after your Mom. She seems like a pretty nice lady. Say, let's ride the merry-go-round. What do you say?"

"Sure, if it'll make you happy."

We queued up for the merry-go-round. There were some nifty horses on it, as well as other animals. A zebra, a tiger, even a small elephant. But when it came our turn to get on, I picked out a bench, about the width of a love seat, with the carved silhouette of a white swan at each end.

"This one OK?" I asked.

"Sure, if you want to ride on a goose. Watch out for the beaks."

We got on, and pretty soon the merry-go-round started up. First slow, then a whole lot faster. The music they were playing — I think it was a banjo concerto of some sort — was kind of loud. I slid over closer to Tracy so she could hear me.

"You know, my little Avocado Éclair, I've been thinking of getting a partner."

"You? Why? You don't have enough business."

"I don't mean that kind of partner." I fumbled in my pocket and got out a velvet-covered box. "I was thinking more along the lines of a wife." I opened the box and handed it to her. "Will you marry me?"

"A diamond ring? How could you afford it?"

"I made a down payment. It's not much of a diamond. It looks like something you'd find when you were sweeping up a diamond cutter's floor."

"No, it doesn't. It's magnificent. It's the biggest diamond I've ever seen. It's brighter than all the carnival lights put together."

"Put it on."

She did, and it was about the right size.

"Well?" I asked.

"Will I marry you? Of course I'll marry you, you big sap."

She kissed me, right there in public, and that's something for Tracy.

We got off the merry-go-round and walked around a little, neither of us talking. We came upon the fortuneteller's booth and Tracy said she wanted her palm read.

"And while I'm in there, don't you dare go watch the belly dancer."

"I won't. All that swaying and gyrating makes me seasick."

243

While Tracy was getting her palm read, I headed back over to the Big Striker. I wanted to take one more shot at it. The burly carny recognized me.

"Back, are you? You better ring that bell this time, bub, or you ain't getting no prizes."

"Don't you worry, I'll ring it."

I gave him the tickets and picked up the mallet. I swung it nice and easy but with some strength behind it. And damned if the bell didn't ring. The line of folks behind me sent up a cheer.

"OK, Sampson, what'll it be?" The carny gestured at his fine array of prizes.

"I'll take what we traded you last time. That plug-ugly monkey with the lop ears."

I think he was glad to get rid of it. I walked back over to the fortuneteller's booth, and Tracy was just coming out. She was looking at her ring and almost bumped into a fat lady holding a baby.

"Say, how'd you get my bunny back?" Tracy asked me as I handed it to her.

"I rang the bell."

"You always ring mine."

We spent another hour or so at the carnival. We rode some more rides, though nothing that went up in the air. We ate some more of what they were calling food. Then we tried out the shooting gallery. Tracy won a kewpie, but I got nothing. They wouldn't let me use my own gun. When we headed for home, Tracy didn't want to drive in the dark, so I drove. Every time we took a curve the fuzzy pink dice hanging from the mirror swayed back and forth.

"So, Tracy, what'd the fortune teller have to say?"

"She told me I was going to marry a tall, dark, handsome man, with lots of money." She scooted closer to me on the seat. "See, I told you those carnival fortune tellers are always wrong. I don't know how they do it."

"Honest to crazy Godfrey!"

END

If you have enjoyed this book, please go to its Amazon book page and leave a short review. It will be most appreciated!

OTHER BOOKS BY THIS AUTHOR:

DEAD MAN LIMPING
[ISBN: 978-1-940469-00-3]

When 1950s private eye Axel Hatchett is hired by
a delectable redhead to turn up her missing husband, Hatchett discovers that the man is not only
still alive, but is armed, probably crazy, and is on a
killing spree that may include Hatchett! But something stinks about this case — big time — and it's
not Hatchett's pet skunk, Ambrosia.

SLAYER IN A GRAY TOUPEE
[ISBN: 978-1-940469-01-0]

Rumpled 1950s sleuth, Axel Hatchett, is sum-
moned to the Flinders Mansion to prevent a mil-
lionaire's threatened murder. After a fierce bliz-
zard knocks out the power and closes the roads,
Hatchett is trapped in the candle-lit mansion with
an eccentric array of terrified guests and servants.
The detective is determined to solve the case, but
his only clue is a sinister gray toupee.

THREE CURSING BIRDS
[ISBN: 978-1-940469-03-4]

When thieves snatch a statue of the bird-headed Egyptian god, Thoth, and drop its owner from a third-story window, 1950s private detective Axel Hatchett is set on their trail. But wait! — there are actually three statues, and one of them may contain a treasure map! Hatchett enlists the aid of his hash-slinging fiancée and a snake-handling English professor to help solve the case of the three cursed birds.

KILLER BEAR FOR HIRE
[ISBN: 978-1-940469-04-1]

In all his years of sleuthing, snarky 1950s private eye Axel Hatchett has never faced a case like this: a bear trained to kill. Hatchett finds himself hunted by a deadly two-legged predator whose bullet comes unnervingly close to Hatchett's new wife, and that has Hatchett seeing red! Armed with a revolver and his caustic wits, Hatchett is out to solve a grizzly killing, or die trying.

BOOK CLUB DISCUSSION QUESTIONS
(For People Who Didn't Skip Over the Dull Parts)

1. Did the main characters change by the end of the book? Do they learn something about themselves? Did you learn something about yourself?

2. What do the characters do? Do they react the way you think you would in a similar situation? Do their actions trouble you? They sure trouble me....

3. Did the story interest you? Has it inspired you to take up a new hobby such as snake breeding?

4. Does the book have a main theme? Many themes? Any theme at all? What's a theme?

5. Did the title of this book create interest for you? Why or why not?

6. Was the ending satisfying? If so, why? If not, why not? Were you hoping for something more like Hamlet where everyone dies at the end?

7. Did this novel change you? Bring on mood swings? Changes in personality?

8. What was the author trying to accomplish (provide entertainment for the reader, deliver a message, rid himself of demons?)

9. Would you buy another novel by this author? Why?

10. Contrast this book with others you have read, for example, books by the same author, or books with a similar approach.

ABOUT THE AUTHOR

Steven LeRoy Nelson is an award-winning
humorist whose short fiction has appeared in
*Alfred Hitchcock Mystery Magazine, Ellery Queen
Mystery Magazine, The Leviathan,* and numerous
other publications.

Visit him at his website at:

www.stevenleroynelson.com